WHO WOULD WANT TO KILL

a lovely, delicate girl like Hope? True, her late father was a monster. True, her former lover was a broken man. True, her current husband was little more than her hired servant. True, her life was little more than a high wire act of deception and betrayal. Still, a broken neck seemed a steep price to pay for one false step.

WHO WOULD WANT TO KILL

a friendly girl like Winnie? True, she was forever prying into forbidden places. True, she turned other people's secrets into her own vicious weapons. True, she gorged herself on envy and untiringly exercised evil. Still, why had curiosity killed this cruel and cunning cat?

WHO WOULD WANT TO KILL

an innocent like Susan?
As far as Susan could see, it could be virtually anyone around her in THE BROWNSTONE HOUSE.

Also by Rae Foley
in Jove/HBJ Editions

**SUFFER A WITCH
WHERE HELEN LIES
PUT OUT THE LIGHT
ONE O'CLOCK AT THE GOTHAM**

RAE FOLEY

THE BROWNSTONE HOUSE

HBJ

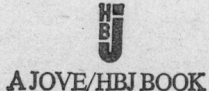

A JOVE/HBJ BOOK

Copyright © 1974 by Rae Foley

Published by arrangement with Dodd, Mead & Company

All rights reserved. No part of this publication may be reproduced or transmitted in any form or by any means, electronic or mechanical, including photocopy, recording or any information storage and retrieval system, without permission in writing from the publisher.

First Jove/HBJ edition published August 1978

Library of Congress Catalog Card Number: 74-3786

Printed in the United States of America

Jove/HBJ books are published by Jove Publications, Inc.
(Harcourt Brace Jovanovich)
757 Third Avenue, New York, N.Y. 10017

*For Jane and Mildred
With warm affection*

Prologue

On a day in July, shortly before the opening of the nominating convention in which he was the leading candidate for the Presidency, as well as the most popular and highly regarded of the younger leaders to emerge in the country, Graham Woods died in his election headquarters with a bullet in his brain.

There was no question about his death. It was suicide. His prints were found on the gun that lay on the floor beside his limp hand. There were two notes on the desk at which he had been sitting. One of them was addressed to his wife and its contents were never disclosed. Their mutual devotion had been well known. After the police had finished with the body and she had attended the funeral service—alone, by request— she walked into the river that wound past his country estate and drowned.

The second letter was addressed to the police and was given full play:

> I am taking my life because—call it pride or vanity or shame or despair—I cannot face the exposure with which I am threatened, and which, in any case, would destroy my effectiveness as a leader of the people. Once in my life I made a bad mistake, due to youth and inexperience. This action has now been unearthed and fully documented and will be used against me if I let my name stand as a candidate for the Presidency. This is the work of men who have found it profitable to destroy my credibility and my value as a trustworthy public servant.

This country is weary of dishonesty on the part of its public servants, whether those whom they have elected or those who work behind the scenes; weary of lies and treachery; weary of chicanery and evasion of the truth. God knows it deserves something better. I believe with all my heart that, in spite of my past error, or perhaps even because of it, I would have been a useful President, with the best interests of the people at heart, but the men who have attacked me are not interested in the integrity of their public officials, only in their willingness to serve private interests.

My beloved wife knows nothing of my past transaction. She has always believed in me. Spare her as much as you can.

The shot that killed Graham Woods may not have been heard round the world but, like a pebble in a still pool, it caused ripples that spread and spread, not only leaving the public stunned and shocked but affecting the lives of a number of individuals. It led, directly or indirectly, to three deaths and, for one, the living death of a life sentence in a penitentiary. It led to the revelation of an organization so corrupt and so widespread that its eventual exposure and the resultant collapse of the whole rotten structure raised a dust like the mushroom cloud over Hiroshima.

It led to the involvement of innocent people who had never exchanged a word with Graham Woods but who, to their own bewilderment, found themselves caught up in the chain reaction that followed his suicide.

It even involved me in a painful and humiliating scandal, repercussions of which I still feel occasionally when someone looks at me on the street, laughs, and says, "Did anyone ever tell you that you resemble the model who was found naked in a bathtub?"

Chapter 1

People don't really change. Not fundamentally. When they surprise us, it is because we failed to recognize their potentialities. The most terrible statement I know is that what happens to us is like us, that we shape our characters and our destinies by the choices we make.

It was when I entered college that I became a part, almost unwittingly, of what Hope Phelps called "The Inseparables." How it came about, I did not know. The three of us were unlike in every possible way: in appearance, in character, in background, in potential future.

Even then Winifred Winston was too stout, too anxious to assure herself that she was getting her fair share out of life. Even then she revealed an almost obsessive curiosity about her fellowmen. Nothing was too trivial to escape her attention, that tireless prying until every detail had been revealed and explained. Even then she ended most of her statements with an "Isn't it?" that demanded an answer.

Even then Hope Phelps was small and blonde and very pretty in a delicate way. Some quality about her made an irresistible appeal to sympathy and one wanted instinctively to protect her, though under her gentleness and her softness there was a vein of iron. Where Winnie looked at life with insatiable curiosity, Hope regarded it with a kind of ironic detachment that sat oddly on her slight shoulders. Even then she betrayed a kind of innate insecurity. She clung to her friends. It was she who had created the bond, or whatever it was, among the three of us, shaping us into a close-knit group.

Hope had a background of money and, through her father, a wide acquaintance with distinguished people. She had the protection of wealth and an assured future, not only because of her father's position but because of Hart Adams, her father's assistant or secretary, or whatever he was, who was her devoted escort and whom, in time, she would marry. It was Hart who escorted her to dances at college or, when in New York, to theaters and night clubs. It was Hart who kept her room filled with flowers and who remembered holidays, not just Christmas and birthdays, but Columbus Day and Hallowe'en and even Veteran's Day. Anything was an excuse for Hart to reveal his unshakable devotion.

Hope received all this lavish homage with her usual gentle irony, but she was so accustomed to it that none of us who knew her well believed she could endure having it withdrawn.

Winnie was constantly trying to find out just how serious Hart's devotion was and whether Hope would marry him. As usual, when she wished to probe a situation, her questions were interminable, with a maddening sort of insistence that was completely impervious to rebuff.

Only once did Hope's patience snap under that constant prod, prod, prod that was Winnie's idea of conversation. "Did you ever hear that curiosity killed the cat?"

Winnie looked at her in wide-eyed surprise, taken aback by the sharpness in the usually gentle voice. "Well, I just like to know. Don't you? That's natural, isn't it?"

"I don't," Hope said dryly, "carry it to the point of listening to other people's phone calls or reading any stray letters one happens to leave lying around."

"Well, I'm sure I didn't think the letter was private or you wouldn't have left it right out on your desk."

I choked and Hope flicked a quick, amused glance at me.

"And as for that telephone call—honestly, you were

talking so loud I couldn't have helped hearing unless I'd gone right out of the room."

"People have been known to do that," Hope informed her, "when someone is having a private conversation."

"I must say I don't see why if there's nothing to hide, nothing to be ashamed of, I mean. And I knew, from the way you spoke, it was your father, so it couldn't be private. Well, could it? So naturally I was interested because he's really an important man. Everyone says so. But why they call him the Gray Eminence I never could find out. His hair is dark, no silver threads."

"Silver threads," Hope said, and she began to laugh.

Winnie was being educated by two uncles who were more dutiful than affectionate and who had made clear to her that after her graduation she was to be on her own and to expect no further assistance from them.

I had an excellent scholarship and a generous check given me by a wealthy and rather silly woman who had bought a portrait I had done of her daughter. As I recall now, it was not a very good painting, though it was the best work I had done up to then. At least it was a faithful likeness and, as the girl died shortly after I had finished it, her mother valued it more highly than it deserved. But even a generous check cannot last forever, and I too was to be on my own when I graduated. It did not occur to me to fear the future. I was young and eager and confident that the world was my oyster. Never having suffered any serious rebuff or disappointment up to that time, this was understandable enough.

Hope never referred to the tremendous difference in our circumstances, but when we visited her father's huge Fifth Avenue apartment, an eighteen-room duplex, her background was necessarily impressed on us. Her father, Marshall Phelps, was an impressive-looking man, tall, well-built, with a fine speaking voice and attractive manners. Like Hope he seemed to take genuine pleasure in making Winnie and me feel at home. He behaved as though it were Hope and not we who should be grateful for our friendship.

We saw more of him during those four long Christmas vacations than might be expected, because he conducted his business, whatever it was, from the huge library on the first floor of the duplex. This, like the rest of the apartment, was impressive in its size and luxury but, unlike the rest, it had a separate entrance to the outside corridor, opening directly on the elevator. People came and went through that door and were not seen in the rest of the apartment. One got the kind of impression that I suppose one has on entering the White House, that great matters were being resolved in that library *cum* office.

When Mr. Phelps appeared among us, he was always affable and he took pains to see that we enjoyed our vacation and seemed eager to oblige us in any possible way. He watched complacently Hart's attentions to his daughter and it was obvious that he approved of them.

Hart never seemed to take his eyes off Hope. He was an attractive young man, the kind who, a couple of generations ago, would have gone from his college football team to selling bonds to his prosperous friends. An early friendship between his father and Mr. Phelps had led the latter to offer him a job, and he had soon become a trusted assistant. Whatever devotion Hart had left from Hope he expended on her father.

On the last Christmas that Winnie and Hope and I spent together, Marshall Phelps gave his daughter an unusual Christmas present—a run-down old brownstone house in the mid-Fifties on the fashionable West Side.

When he saw that she was more surprised than elated, he smiled. "I don't expect you to live in it; I trust that you will live here as long as I am around. But I know what is going on. Practically that whole block has been sold and a thirty-story building is to be erected. This house is the only holdout and as it is in the very middle of the block, it is extremely important. Don't sell it now, Hope. Keep it for two years and you'll get your own price."

"What shall I do with it? Rent it?"

"The cost of necessary repairs and decoration would

make that impractical. No, let it stand as it is. Believe me, it will prove to be more valuable than you know." And he laughed.

That was the last Christmas, as I have said, that Winnie and Hope and I had spent in the Fifth Avenue apartment, and even my then our friendship was becoming a trifle frayed, though none of us seemed to be aware of it. During our last college year we had all enrolled for an art seminar conducted by Lawrence Garland, one of the most popular young instructors on the faculty.

I'd seen him on the campus, of course, walking with his long, swift strides, apparently unaware of the admiring and wistful glances cast at him by his students. I say *apparently* because he must, in his thirty years, have become aware that he had a quality that made him attractive to women, though he wasn't particularly goodlooking, a big and rangy man with a slightly crooked nose and a delightful smile.

At that time he was, in an unstressed way, mildly pleased with himself and his world. He gave the impression of being superbly confident that he could cope with any situation that might arise. A saving grace was his nice sense of humor, an ability to laugh at himself, and a deprecating manner that was very winning when he caught himself being pontifical, a trap into which even the best of lecturers are bound to fall from time to time.

Where the women students were concerned, he had developed a policy of noninvolvement. He was careful to display no personal interest in them; he always managed to wedge himself into a table filled with faculty members in the cafeteria; and he went striding through the campus, looking neither to right nor to left.

It was not, however, Lawrence Garland's legendary charm that attracted me to the seminar. I was an art student, studying to become an illustrator. Actually I was the only serious art student in the seminar, the others being equally divided between those with a desire for culture and those with a desire to meet the young instructor.

Winnie signed up for the course because she was hell-bent on getting the most out of her college education, and that included a heavy dose of culture. No man ever had a more tractable pupil. She admired what he admired, she sneered at what he disliked. She studied each painting with painstaking care but without delight, accepting or rejecting in accordance with the dictates of the master.

Why Hope was taking the course, she did not say. Hope did not often explain herself. Whether, even then, she was attracted to Lawrence Garland I do not know. She seemed to view the paintings as she did her fellow-men—with ironic detachment.

I suppose it was inevitable that all three of us should fall in love with Lawrence Garland. As this was par for the course I did not, for a moment, dream that anything serious could come of the situation. He was an inevitable part of our education.

My first meeting with him outside the classroom was a head-on collision when we were caught in a sudden, torrential rainstorm and ran into each other as both of us were trying to seek the shelter of a narrow doorway. After I had pulled my face out of his coat and he had steadied me, we laughed and then he held the door open for me. We found ourselves in a little Italian restaurant with steam rising from kettles of boiling spaghetti and from our wet clothing. There were only a dozen tables in the little family-run business. As the storm showed no indication of letting up and we couldn't go on standing there, dripping on the floor, he suggested, "It's a bit early to eat, but we might as well stay here, don't you think? Anyhow, the food is good and ample and cheap, which is a consideration."

He didn't wait for my consent but selected a table and ordered for both of us, including a bottle of red wine. His manner was a shade dictatorial for my taste, but he did not seem to be aware of it. He was, I thought, so accustomed to having his own way that he took it for granted, and though this annoyed me, I was in no position to cavil, not only because I could not go out in the rain without being soaked to the skin but because I lacked the confidence that comes with knowing one looks one's best. I definitely did not. My hair hung in wet strands over my forehead and dripped down the back of my neck. My dress began to shrink as soon as it got wet and clung more and more revealingly to my body. My shoes oozed wetness. I couldn't have looked worse, which put me at a disadvantage.

While the papa set breadsticks and a carafe of red wine on the table, his daughter, with an admiring look at Lawrence—what was it about the man?—put bowls of minestrone before us, and the son, busy stirring the spaghetti, gave us a beaming smile, while the mamma, her watchful eye on chickens revolving on the rotisserie, seemed to join in the general aura of welcome that surrounded us.

"You're Susan Lockwood."

I nodded, taken aback that Dr. Garland had remembered me.

"You're the only one in that seminar who knows what I am talking about—or cares really. You're studying art, aren't you? Well, actually, I know you are. And very good, too, according to old Waldron. Developing a style of your own."

"I want to be an illustrator," and I gave him a half-defiant look. "Commercial art, of course."

"Well," he said mildly, "it's nice to be able to eat regularly and it needn't preclude doing other work, need it?"

"I'll never be first-rate as a painter; I haven't anything beyond a certain facility."

"That's not what Waldron said. A good eye and a style of your own."

"Slick," I said gloomily.

He grinned. "In spite of all the efforts of all the critics people still prefer to recognize what's in a painting. Stupid of them, no doubt, but there it is."

With the exception of another couple taking refuge, like us, from the storm, and a large family party well known to the management and welcomed vociferously, we had the place to ourselves. The rain continued to fall in buckets, the streets were wet and windswept, with the gutters already overflowing into treacherous pools at street crossings, so we lingered on. Lawrence ordered brandy with our coffee and we sat talking idly, looking now and then at the table with the Italians, who seemed more vividly alive than other people, enjoying themselves immensely.

It was all so easy and natural that I forgot how awful I must look, though I knew that when my hair dried it curled up as tightly as Topsy's unless firmly controlled, and that thrice-accursed dress—Hope had warned me that it was poor economy to buy cheap material—was shrinking by the minute. Just my luck that we were in a brightly lighted restaurant so that every line of my body was revealed almost as clearly as though I had worn no dress at all. Lawrence did not observe this phenomenon, which relieved me. At least it should have.

He told me that he liked teaching; there was nothing he would rather do.

"Except paint?"

"I do some work on the side, big stuff mostly, murals. Don't ask me why. I don't know. I seem to need a lot of space in which to say anything."

"But there's so little market for murals!"

"Which is why it's a damned good thing I like teaching. This is your last year, isn't it? Why did you bother with the seminar? You must know most of that stuff. We hold it chiefly for people who want an easy course or want to be taught what to say about art. Not think, you understand. Just say."

I laughed. "Like Winnie Winston?"

"Is she the stout little number with an echo instead of a voice? And that infuriating way of following up every comment with 'Isn't it?' So damned insistent."

"Poor Winnie! How unkind of you to make fun of your most docile pupil."

"Winnie the Pooh. Don't worry about her. She'll always come out, one way or another."

As I raised inquiring eyebrows, he said lightly, "Our Winnie the Pooh has some very unengaging traits. Looks at other people's notes. Picks up letters. Pawed over some papers on my desk the other afternoon after the seminar. I went back to collect my notes and there was our Winnie looking at everything in sight."

"Oh, dear! But she doesn't mean any harm, you know. She simply has an overwhelming sense of curiosity."

"If she doesn't learn to curb it, she is going to find herself in trouble one of these days." He sounded unexpectedly tart.

"But she's harmless."

"Why you should be defending the indefensible, I can't imagine. She's hardly your type."

"Actually we are very good friends."

"I can't figure out why."

Neither had I until then. I realized now for the first time that it was Hope who had drawn us both into her orbit. "I hardly know," I admitted, "but somehow the three of us, Winnie and Hope and I—"

"Hope?"

"She's in the seminar too. Hope Phelps. A pretty girl with blond hair."

"Oh, the lass with the delicate air."

"Well, yes. The three of us usually sit together."

"I hadn't noticed her especially. It's a big group. Too big."

But he had noticed me. He had even bothered to look up my record and talk to my art instructor. I would have been less than human if I had not felt a glow of gratitude that it was I whom Lawrence Garland had signaled out and not Hope, who was so much prettier.

"She's a lovely person," I said, "sweet and defenseless and generous. I can't tell you how generous. Winnie and I are always, somehow, on the receiving end. It makes for rather a one-sided friendship."

"I shouldn't think so. You have more life in you than a dozen Hopes. I suspect she gets a lot more out of

17

you than you do out of her. But when you speak of her, you have something in your voice, as though she were special."

"I suppose everyone feels like that about Hope. I don't quite know why. Not protective, exactly. Well, perhaps that is it. Tempering the wind."

Lawrence was not impressed. "That must be quite a line she has." He sounded sardonic. "I'll have to take another look at the girl. What is her problem, neglect or being misunderstood or ill-treated by her nearest and dearest?"

I laughed. "Far from it. She is surrounded by adoring people: her father, his assistant whom she will probably marry, her friends. Her father is Marshall Phelps, you know."

His brows shot up. "Not the Gray Eminence himself?"

"That's the one, but I've never understood why." I added in some surprise, "You know I don't have any idea what his position really is."

"Neither does anyone else. He's the track-coverer-upper to end track-coverer-uppers."

I leaped to Mr. Phelps's defense, though heaven knows he needed none from me. "Whatever that is supposed to mean! He's a very important man, gracious and generous, devoted to his daughter, kind to her friends—"

"My, my! He certainly sold you a bill of goods."

"What makes you dislike him so much?"

Angry eyes met mine squarely. "It's not merely the man himself, it's the kind of person he is, what he stands for. I don't like king-makers. I don't like the ringmaster who cracks his whip. I don't like the powers behind the throne. I don't like having to see grinning puppets posture and mouth high-falutin remarks while someone else is pulling the strings and putting the words into their mouths."

After a moment, while I gaped at him in astonishment, Lawrence added harshly, "And it's my personal belief that Phelps is the man who forced Graham

Woods to put a bullet through his head, and to my mind Woods was the finest and most honorable public servant we've had in this country in a decade."

"That's a monstrous thing to suggest! I've known Mr. Phelps for nearly four years and spent weeks in his New York apartment. It's preposterous for you to be trying to turn him into a villain."

"So heated? He's really turned you on, hasn't he?"

"A man doesn't inspire the kind of devotion he gets from his daughter and his assistant, the people who know him best, and he doesn't hold the kind of position Mr. Phelps does in the public eye by false pretenses."

"Does he not? You haven't really seen a large cross section of the human race, have you? Such illusions should be cherished."

He was laughing at me, but I chose to ignore it. I looked at my watch. "Heavens, we have been here for four hours and the rain has stopped."

"So it has," he said in surprise. "Wait here for ten minutes while I pick up my car and I'll drive you back to your dormitory."

"You don't need to bother," I said hypocritically.

"You have a treat in store for you, Sue," he said, and I blinked in surprise. Four hours ago he had identified me vaguely as a student named Susan Lockwood and now I had become Sue without any transition at all. "This is an experience you shouldn't miss."

When he drove up in front of the restaurant, I broke into laughter. He was driving the largest, the highest, and certainly the oldest car I'd ever been in, with an astronomical number of miles on it.

"Meet the Queen Mary," he said proudly as he helped me in. It started with only the faintest of protests and moved at a stately twenty miles an hour. Without asking for directions, Lawrence pulled up before my dormitory.

"How did you know which one it is?" I asked.

"Oh, I've seen you go in and out. Can't miss that black hair and the way it curls up as though it had a separate life of its own. I've always wanted to touch it." He stretched out a hand and rested it lightly on my head. "Mmh—soft as silk, too."

He got out and opened the door. "You have to give it a hard bang or it won't close, but if you bang too hard, it falls off. Good night, Sue. I'll get in touch tomorrow. No, damn it, there's a faculty meeting I have to attend. Well, next day then. We've got to make up for lost time. School's out in another five weeks."

Without giving me a chance to collect my scattered wits, he waved and then went back to climb into the Queen Mary and make a regal departure down the street, leaving me in a glow that could have warmed an igloo.

Chapter 2

For some reason which I did not attempt to analyze, I said nothing about that meeting to Winnie or Hope. But, as I might have known, Winnie heard of it from some girl who was coming in late just as Lawrence delivered me to the dormitory. At once a barrage of questions poured from her. How had I happened to meet Dr. Garland? Had I ever been out with him before? Why hadn't I said a single word about it? What kind of person was he when he wasn't teaching? With that smile and that—oh, you know what I mean—I should think you'd be careful about being seen with him. It might start people talking. You know how they do.

"She knows," Hope said. "For heaven's sake, can't she have a single date without starting all this commotion?"

"Well, it's different with you and Hart," Winnie explained. "We know all about Hart, but Dr. Garland—"

"You'd better tell her all," Hope advised me in resignation, "if you expect to have any peace. Sometimes I wonder, Winnie, why Sue and I haven't strangled you."

So, because it was easier, I explained how I had happened to run, literally, into Lawrence Garland and how we had had dinner together in the little Italian restaurant because it was raining too hard to leave, and that was all there had been to it, I added not quite truthfully.

For once Winnie was satisfied, but Hope gave me a quick, sidelong look. "I was worried, Sue, when you weren't back for dinner, afraid you'd been caught in the rain. How nice that you should have had such a pleasant experience."

"You were right about that green dress, Hope," I said in an attempt to change the focus of interest. "Wait until you see how it shrank. It's practically indecent. I'll never be able to wear it again."

Winnie laughed. "Well, heaven knows it's your own fault. Hope warned you and warned you."

In the next three weeks I saw Larry about every day. We went back to the Italian restaurant for dinner and were aware that the whole family was watching the progress of a love affair with sympathetic interest. And yet it wasn't really a love affair. On our dates Larry never spoke of love. Our talk was as light and casual as it had been at our first meeting except that each time we revealed a little more about ourselves. I remember chiefly how relaxed it always was, how much we laughed, how increasingly eager we were to pour out the events, trivial for the most part, of the intervening days. We never discussed the future. The only time that concerned us, at least that concerned Larry, was now, the present moment, the next date.

In the seminar there was no apparent change in our relationship. Larry never signaled me out in any way, but occasionally there was a swift, almost involuntary, exchange of glances, as when Winnie would make one of her statements, followed by the insistent "Isn't it?" demanding an answer.

On a May day, when laurel was in bloom, Larry parked the Queen Mary and we walked through a little woods, strolling aimlessly. Larry took my hand and held it casually as we walked. Unexpectedly he laughed. "I love to watch your expression. I always have the feeling that you are waiting breathlessly for something strange and wonderful to happen."

"You make me sound like a child waiting for Christmas morning," I protested.

"Something like that."

"But doesn't everyone look forward to what may happen next?"

"Not me. Or to speak more in keeping with my august position, not I. My life is planned down to the last detail. I've got the job I like best, and enough leisure to do some painting of my own. In the summers I travel, tourist class, to see the museums of the world. I earn enough to live on but, of course, I don't need much. I have no extravagant tastes. I rent the loft in that old warehouse on Mill Street, which has a good north light and plenty of space for murals, and it's cheap." He added with a rueful grin, "You'd hate it, Sue. There is a minimum of secondhand furniture and a once-a-week cleaning woman who is slapdash, to say the least. I own a few good paintings, an excellent record player, a fair library of records, and a few hundred books. That's the lot. As you can see, I have gathered no moss. I'm the frugal type, which accounts for the Queen Mary and the restaurants I take you to."

"Oh," I was surprised into saying, "I thought that was because you didn't want anyone to know you were seeing me. You've got that reputation, you know. Hard-to-get Garland."

"For God's sake." Then he laughed. "Well, I suppose it's true in a way. I never wanted to get involved with any of my students, to get involved with anyone who might threaten my independence, until the day you came into the seminar with that winged walk and your eager face, looking as though you expected something wonderful was going to happen."

"You make me sound like a fool," I complained.

"You," he told me, his voice still light, casual, "are a darling. You are also the kind of girl to upset a man's best-laid plans—and make him like it." We turned back toward the Queen Mary. "Someday I wish you'd come see that place of mine." He grinned. "No etchings! Word of honor. Just so you can get an all-round view of the subject."

Then, as though to prove to both of us that there was no serious intention behind his words, he launched into a hilarious and probably libelous account of the trials and transgressions of a member of the faculty and his dubious marital status.

II

That was the last date I had with Lawrence Garland. The next night Hope came to my room after I had gone to bed. She sat curled up in my easy chair, wearing one of her exquisite robes, this one of peach-colored velvet. Her big eyes were shadowed and she was very pale. The hand she laid on my arm shocked me because it was so cold.

"Sue," she said. "Oh, Sue!" Then she crumpled in a heap and began to sob. She had always been so completely in control of herself that I was shaken by her outbreak. At last I got her to drink a little water, bathed her face, and applied witch hazel pads to her eyes.

After a while she began to talk quietly. "I'm so sorry. So sorry. I didn't mean to do that, but all of a sudden it was too much to bear all by myself."

That afternoon, she said, she had gone to New York to see her doctor. "But you've met him. Dr. Partridge. You went to him last year when you cut your arm so badly." There had been something wrong for a long time—she tired quickly and got out of breath—but she had ignored it. "Hoping it would go away," she said with an uncertain smile.

But it wasn't going to go away. Her heart had been badly impaired during a bout of rheumatic fever when she was traveling with her father and there was no adequate medical advice available. The doctor had told her bluntly that there was no cure. All she could do was take reasonable care of herself and avoid physical and emotional strain. She might live for another year, or with luck, for two.

There was nothing I could say because there is no answer to doom. There are no stupid lies or false cheer that a girl like Hope would accept.

At last she said, sounding exhausted, "So I've been

thinking about the future, my future, I mean, and wondering what I could do with that time, so little time in which to cram a whole life! And there is only one thing I want, only one thing in the world that would make me happy, that could make up—almost—"

The moments dragged on and all at once my heart accelerated its beat. I was afraid. I didn't want to know what it was that would make Hope happy and compensate for a tragically curtailed life.

"I'm in love with Lawrence Garland," she said at last. "I fell in love with him the first week of the seminar. Oh, he's never paid any attention to me. I think I knew before you did that he was attracted to you. And I've seen the change in you—the glow. I've seen the way you catch each other's eyes during the seminar, almost as though you had touched each other!"

I don't think I could have spoken then to save my life.

At last Hope sat up, the peach-velvet shimmering under the light. She dropped the witch hazel pads on the rug and she met my eyes levelly. "Sue, I have only a short time, a couple of years at most, maybe a few months. Let me have Lawrence Garland. Afterwards —you can have him for the rest of your life, but let me have him now."

"But, Hope," I began helplessly. I grabbed at a straw. "What about Hart?"

She shrugged. "Oh, Hart," she said wearily. "Well, Sue?"

"But it isn't a question of giving him up. He has never asked me to marry him. He has never even said he loves me."

"Oh!" She brightened. "Oh, I'm so glad. Then he doesn't really care. All I ask you, Sue, is please don't see him for a while. Just give me a chance."

"But if he doesn't—" My voice trailed off. The lass with the delicate air. Lovely and sweet as she was, Hope wasn't Larry's type. I was sure of that. And he had an almost obsessive hatred and distrust of her father.

"Leave that to me. Without the kind of competition

you can put up, I'll be all right." Hope got briskly to her feet, the color back in her cheeks, her eyes shining. "Leave that to me," she repeated.

III

Hope's wedding to Lawrence Garland, early in September, was a brilliant affair. She was attended by Winnie, stout and perspiring in green satin that was horribly unbecoming. The end of our college association had not ended Winnie's hold on Hope. With that devastating perseverance of hers she managed to see her at least a couple of times a week. Larry's best man, unbelievably, was Hart Adams, looking like death. Hope herself was enchanting in an exquisite white wedding dress, radiantly happy as she came down the aisle on Larry's arm. In formal morning clothes, in contrast to the slacks and sweaters he wore on the campus, he seemed like a stranger, grave and remote, his manner toward his young bride gentle and protective. By chance his eyes met mine for a fleeting moment and then passed on, apparently without recognition. I felt a sharp stab of pain but, after all, I had asked for it.

From the time I had stopped seeing him, Hope and I, by mutual agreement, never discussed him. In fact, I saw her only a couple of times during that summer before her marriage. Marshall Phelps had, with his customary kindness, found a job for Winnie in the office of one of his business acquaintants, a prominent contractor. He offered to provide for me, too, but, in spite of Hope's protests and insistence, I was determined to forge for myself. By sheer luck I acquired a job for which I certainly was not looking. I had attended a style show and sat more or less idly sketching the models as they went past. As it happened, the store manager was sitting beside me. He bought the sketches for use in newspaper advertising and then took me aback.

"Have you ever thought of doing any modeling yourself?"

"Never."

"You have the build for it and the sculptural sort of face that helps set off good clothes and furs, probably sports wear and certainly evening gowns. You're tall enough to display clothes well and, of course, you have a good voice and diction. Too many models ruin the effect as soon as they open their mouths. You have that necessary touch of class."

I laughed at the time, but I was dangerously short of money and a week later I went to see the manager and worked out an arrangement by which I would do modeling part-time, enough at least to pay for food and incidentals, and still have leisure for illustrating if I could get any commissions.

And there again I ran into unexpected luck. After making the wearisome rounds of publishers' offices, I met an editor who gave me a chance to do a book jacket. He liked it, other people liked it, and he introduced me to Roger Mullen, a happy-go-lucky young man with careless charm, an acute eye for the unusual, and an ability to write vivid prose. The idea was that, if we liked each other and could work out some sort of mutually satisfactory arrangement, I would illustrate some offbeat travel books he had contracted to write.

We liked each other at once and made plans over cocktails, so it was Roger who helped me to get over the worst of the summer and fall. He was a cheerful companion, amusing to be with, fun to talk to, and the work itself was absorbing. The only problem was his one-track determination to make love to me and my equally firm determination to keep our relationship on an impersonal basis. Inevitably this resulted in an emotional tug-of-war in which I ceded more than I liked and less than he liked.

As an inevitable result of our divergent interests The Inseparables went their separate ways. I had wondered, somewhat wryly, at the speed with which Hope had won Larry's devotion and apparently overcome his profound distrust of her father. I wondered even more when I encountered a former classmate who told me that Dr. Garland had resigned from the faculty and was going to run an art gallery on Fifty-seventh Street, which Marshall Phelps had bought and given his daughter as a wedding present. The classmate who told me added with a grin, "Hope remembers Dr. Garland's devastating effect on his students. She seems to be eliminating the competition with a ruthless hand. Like father, like daughter. Marshall Phelps has a reputation for paying for what he wants and discarding what he does not want. I never really trusted that velvet glove of Hope's, though, as I recall, you were buddies."

The next surprise was learning that Hope and Larry had moved into the Fifth Avenue apartment owned by Marshall Phelps after their return from the honeymoon. Now and then I could not help wondering whether that apartment, spacious as it was, had room enough in which to paint murals. Or perhaps murals, like the teaching job he loved, had gone by the board. Anyhow, there was, I remembered, no north light in that apartment.

It was Winnie, of course, her eyes glittering with curiosity and malice, who reported that Hart Adams still kept his room at the apartment. Tough as things were for me, my position was a lot easier than that of Hart Adams. To have to be a daily witness to the happiness of a honeymoon couple, a happiness from which I was excluded, was something I could not have borne.

On a scorching day in August, shortly before the wedding, during one of those heat waves that can be so devastating and exhausting on Manhattan where the steel buildings never really cool off at night, I was working at my drawing board, stripped down to halter and shorts, when Hope came to see me, blond hair shining, eyes alight, the picture of health in a sleeveless white dress with a pearl necklace and a tiny diamond on her engagement finger which she wore as proudly as though it were the Kohinoor. As usual she was carrying an enormous handbag.

"Sue! Oh, Sue!" Her face twisted in dismay at the breathless heat in the room. I could not use an electric fan because it blew my papers. She ran across the room holding out both hands. "Oh, Sue, it's heaven to see you. I've missed you terribly."

"But—"

"Oh, I know," she agreed. "I suppose it is better—for everyone—but just the same—" She broke off and I followed her eyes to the desk, on which I had placed a framed sketch I had done of Larry. She wrenched her eyes away. "Do you still—" She broke off that phrase too. Then she sat on the couch that converted into my bed at night. "Sue, I want you to do something for me."

There's nothing more I have to give, I thought bitterly, and then noticed the glow in her face, the sparkle in her eyes. I had given her the possibility of happiness, so bitterness faded in the protective tenderness everyone felt for Hope.

"You remember," she said abruptly, "last Christmas my father gave me a brownstone house in the mid-Fifties on the West Side. It had been converted into apartments, you know, one to a floor. I've been thinking and thinking. Sue, I want you to take one of those apartments. Please!" She threw out a hand before I could protest. "Please! I've talked to Dad about it and he thinks it will be perfect. There's some legal tangle, I don't know what, and it would be better to have an apartment occupied. The place may not be fashionable, but it's a lot better than this. And," she rushed on, "we're giving up the Long Island house because Dad has so little time to go out there and Larry plans to keep the art gallery open on Saturdays, so there is no sense in having the house stand vacant. And there's so much furniture to dispose of that we'll pick out what you need for the apartment. And the brownstone is within walking distance of that store where you model, and it's a floor through so at least there would be cross ventilation. And naturally it would be rent-free."

"No!" The cry of protest came out more emphatically than I had intended.

Hope's eyes opened wider, a startled expression in them. I saw the pulse beating in her throat. A half-frightened question hovered on her lips. "You mean that you won't take anything from me, that you still—" And again her eyes were drawn, as by a magnet, to the sketch of Larry laughing back from my desk.

This was what the doctor had warned against, this kind of emotional turmoil. I took a long steadying breath, and then I said, "I only meant—it's so much. It's too much."

At once the glow came back to her face. "Oh, I'm glad, so terribly glad. Dad is checking on the electricity and the plumbing. There's only one problem. Each apartment has a fireplace, but the chimneys are in bad condition, not properly insulated or something, so don't try to light a fire or the whole place could go up and Dad would be in trouble over evasion of fire laws or something. Okay?"

It wasn't okay, of course. I hated it. To take that apartment, rent-free, plus furniture, was like accepting payment for having relinquished Larry—that is, if I had ever had him. But I tried to accept with as good a grace as I could so as not to destroy Hope's happiness.

This became even more difficult when Winnie, learning as she inevitably would from Hope what had been done for me, at once put in her claim for a similar apartment. Not long after I was established on the second floor, Winnie took the apartment on the third.

As a wedding present I mailed the sketch of Larry to Hope. It was easier to relinquish it than to keep it. I was never one to be satisfied with the shadow instead of the substance, being no Lady of Shalott, and the clean break was more bearable because I was working hard, keeping almost feverishly busy.

The modeling proved to be more tiring than I had foreseen, but I loved the clothes and the management was pleased with me. "People look at you and think they'll look the same," said the buyer with a sardonic expression. "I hear you're in line for a raise or at least a commission on what you manage to sell, and we've never hired a model who put over clothes the way you do."

And the illustrating job went on. I enjoyed my work and the gay evenings with Roger, though too often they ended in an undignified struggle to foil his determination to make love to me.

"Why not?" he asked reasonably enough. "You are free, white, and twenty-one. You can't expect to remain celibate all your life. Too much waste of good material. And here I am—"

"And there you'll stay," I said, laughing, and pushed him out of the apartment. But it was getting to be a bit of a strain.

Aside from the fact that I avoided walking past the art gallery on Fifty-seventh Street, I believed that I had recovered entirely from my infatuation for Larry. At least I thought so until the day when I saw him standing on the far side of Madison Avenue, waiting for a light to change, his topcoat open, no hat as usual, frowning a little into the light. My heart beat so hard I could hardly breathe. Instinctively I turned and began to walk rapidly down Madison Avenue, almost running. I knew then that I had not got over him.

Because we kept different hours, I saw comparatively little of Winnie. Now and then, through the fireplace flue, I heard her television set, which she always turned too loud. Now and then I heard her trip over a hole in the carpeting on the stairs. Now and then we met on the stairs, bringing home groceries, or at the row of mailboxes in the vestibule.

Winnie was completely fascinated by her job. "You have no idea," she explained, and of course I hadn't. A routine office job seemed to me far from exciting. "You have no idea what goes on in business. It opened my eyes, I can tell you." I wondered whether her boss had yet discovered her penchant for going through other people's private papers.

I tried to pick up my mail at times when she was unlikely to be around, for she was still determined to discover the contents of any letter I received, or at least to find out who the sender might be.

During one of these chance mailbox encounters Winnie spoke of Hope, her eyes searching my face as she did so. I wondered then how much she had guessed about the break between Larry and me and his turning so soon to Hope.

"I had dinner last night with Hope." Winnie corrected herself. "I should say with the Garlands. Hope was asking about you. Said she'd be looking in at that store where you model before long as she and Dr. Garland are going abroad on a buying trip for the gallery."

"Oh?"

Winnie smiled. "I guess Hope had her reasons for inviting me. She doesn't ask you any more, does she?

I started to open a letter with an air of great absorption though it was only an appeal for funds from my college.

"Well"—Winnie let the amusement show through— "I knew why she'd asked me, all right. I just happened to see her husband, her bridegroom really, having lunch in a cheap little restaurant over on Third Avenue. I was passing when they went in."

"They?"

"This gorgeous blonde. My dear!" Winnie was openly delighted. "I thought I owed it to Hope to see what was going on, so I went in too. They never noticed me, their heads together, talking as fast as they could. Then the place started to thin out so I figured I'd better leave. I dropped Hope a note. I thought I owed her that. So that's why she asked me to dinner, of course, to show me how sound her marriage was."

I had been too stupid before to see that Winnie had never been devoted to Hope. She hated her. Hated and envied her, jealous of her prettiness and her possessions and her famous and influential father, envious of that apartment on Fifth Avenue. And, recalling Hope's tragedy and her infinite kindness to Winnie, I was so angry that I had to fight for control. What construction Winnie put on my enforced silence I don't know, but it was undoubtedly the worst.

"I had been wondering," she said spitefully, "how long that combination was going to last, keeping an attractive man like Dr. Garland tied to her, even with being able to live free at that swell apartment and having the art gallery and all. Hope is pretty enough, I'll give her that, but she hasn't what it takes to hold a man like her husband." Winnie gave me a knowing look. "You're the one I'd have put my money on to get him. I've always wondered what happened between you two."

I'll bet you have, I thought savagely. "Look here, Winnie. Hope is the most generous girl I know and the best friend either of us has ever had. Why, the very apartments we are living in she gave us rent-free. And that fur coat you are wearing—I remember her giving it to you last winter."

"Well, I declare, Sue, the way you take me up! I just love Hope. But so far as this house is concerned, Mr. Phelps thought it was better for some reason to have people living here. I heard him say so to Hart. That poor mutt! And as for the coat, I can remember how she told me that it was too small for me but it might tempt me to reduce. Hope is not as saintly as you and Hart think she is, or her precious father either. I could tell you a few things about him you'd hardly believe. Did you ever stop to wonder what kind of business he is in? You should get a line on some of the stuff in the files in his library sometime. That would open your eyes."

I started to go upstairs to get away from that venomous tongue. "At least I hope you found that the marriage was still standing on firm ground."

"Oh, yes, yes." Winnie's voice trailed off. "Well, I don't know. He was sweet to her as he always is, as though she was an invalid who had to be taken care of."

As she is, I thought with a stab of pity, and then and there I almost broke down and betrayed Hope's secret to Winnie. I would have if I hadn't realized that, sooner or later, she would find some malicious use for that piece of information.

"I don't know," Winnie went on. "It was a kind of uncomfortable evening. Strained, sort of. Mr. Phelps kept looking at Hart and Hart never took his eyes off Hope, like a whipped dog, and Hope was sort of watching her husband and he was watching Mr. Phelps. Everyone seemed to be watching everyone else. It was," she repeated, "uncomfortable. I must say that for once I was glad to leave."

She came up the stairs behind me. "If I were Hope's husband, I'd watch my step. There was trouble brewing in that place last night."

Chapter 3

But the trouble, when it came a week later, did not involve Lawrence Garland. A maid entering the library in the Fifth Avenue apartment discovered that the lights were on and Marshall Phelps was lying with his head on the desk, one arm stretched out across it, the other hanging at his side. At first she believed he had fallen asleep, but it was he, and not Hope, after all, who had succumbed to a heart attack.

Television, radio, and newspapers hummed with the story. Hope, all during the eulogies delivered by distinguished men at the memorial services, stood up, I noticed with relief, surprisingly well. She was colorless, with a curious rigidity about her face, nostrils pinched, lips pressed hard together. But she did not collapse. She did not even cry. As the impressively long cortege started to the cemetery, following the hearse and the massed flowers, she sat with Larry in a kind of frozen grief. I had never before realized the strength of the bond between father and daughter.

My flowers and letter of sympathy were acknowledged by a card of thanks. Nothing more.

And then, a scant week after the funeral, the first rumblings were heard. Rumors that appeared as the faintest of hints became cautious speculation, and then all the fabric that Marshall Phelps had built began to crumble. The man who had been eulogized as a great citizen, praised even by the President of the United States, was discovered to have spun a tangled web of intrigue, chicanery, blackmail, and bribery, whose repercussions reached into major industries and even into the government itself.

No one seemed to know from whom the first hints of the situation came. Hart Adams was in a state of shock, so stunned by the disclosure of his idol's dishonor that he seemed unable to function intelligently. A conspiracy of silence was set up among the heads of the various groups that had been a part of the strange organization Phelps had built. No one admitted knowing anything. Memories proved to be as erratic and unreliable as those of the reluctant witnesses in the Watergate scandals. The police and, before long, the Treasury, the Federal Bureau of Investigation, and the district attorney's office hunted and investigated and interviewed, but no one admitted anything. The impression given an outraged public was that none of Mr. Phelps's associates had had the slightest knowledge of what they were doing, a state of innocence, as one caustic editorial commented, unequalled since the Fall.

The discovery of the immensity of the graft existing in the country had left the public in a state of shell shock and provided fuel for the malcontents who took instant advantage of it to proclaim that not merely Phelps and his organization but the whole Establishment was corrupt and always had been. Implications, which rapidly became accusations, that Marshall Phelps had been behind the threats leading to the suicide of Graham Woods aroused the people to a state of frustrated rage, frustrated because there was no one on whom to vent their wrath.

I wondered how Larry felt about this disclosure that his father-in-law had indeed been responsible for the destruction of Graham Wood's career. At this juncture there would be small satisfaction in saying "I told you so," and I was sure he had never said so to Hope. She would have forgiven him anything but criticism of her adored father.

Little by little the facts so carefully guarded in the past began to come to light. Phelps's financial affairs were hopelessly tangled. The Treasury boys muttered about income tax evasion over the years, but it was impossible to get hold of anything like proof. The man who had lived so extravagantly appeared to have no tangible assets except for the Fifth Avenue apartment, which he owned. There was no trace of any money except for a modest checking account from which he paid household expenses and salaries for his staff. There was no indication of how he had ever acquired any money. The man who had influenced presidential elections and engineered vast government contracts to industry, the man whose circle of friends extended into almost every field of human endeavor, appeared to have parleyed effrontery and sheer bluff into great power. He had earned the name of Gray Eminence and now had even been stripped of the Emperor's new clothes.

And then Hart Adams revealed that, on the morning after Mr. Phelps's death, the library door opening on the outside corridor had been found unlocked. The room had been searched. Papers that should have been in the files were missing. According to Phelps's valet, his bedroom too had been searched, neatly but thoroughly.

But this time it came hardly as a surprise when an anonymous letter to the FBI suggested that Marshall Phelps had been murdered.

According to the autopsy report, there had been no wound inflicted by gun or knife, no sign of a blow, no poison or drug of any kind, no indication of anything except that his heart had failed suddenly and without warning. True, he had seemed to be in superb health. He had always taken great care of himself, exercised regularly at a gymnasium, and sparred with a young bantamweight prize fighter in order to keep in condition. Still, hearts do stop without warning. There was no proof either way. On the whole, the growing concensus of opinion was that Marshall Phelps had been lucky to die when he did, by whatever means, and to escape the scandal caused by the revelation of his tangled affairs and his criminal activities.

With the widening of the inquiry, not only such business associates as could be traced but Hart and Hope and even Larry were under close questioning by the various forces of the law. When I read that, and I seemed to live on newspapers at that time, I was in a panic. Surely they must know of Hope's precarious health. Such shocks as the death of her father and the subsequent disclosure of his dishonor could easily cut short the life that was destined to be so heartbreakingly short anyhow.

On a gray December day when I had no modeling to do, I finished a batch of drawings, put them carefully in a big portfolio, and started out to deliver them to the editor. As I opened the front door, Hope looked up, startled.

"Hope!" I looked at the pinched face from which all the color, all the gaiety, all the happiness had drained. Her deep mourning, dress and hat and coat, made her appear even more frail, almost haggard. As usual she carried an enormous handbag. I put my arms around her. "Hope!"

For a moment she clung to me and then she freed herself gently. She looked at the portfolio. "Are you going out?"

"It doesn't matter. There's no hurry about these. I'm well ahead of schedule. Come up."

She hesitated, revealing a new diffidence. "Are you sure?"

"Of course I'm sure. You're chilled, and no wonder on a bleak day like this. We'll have some coffee to warm you up."

She followed me up the stairs, tripping on the hole in the worn carpeting. "Heavens, is that still there?" When I had unlocked the door, she looked around her. "What a nice job you've made of it!"

I laughed. "Considering that not only the apartment but the furniture belongs to you—"

"But you've transformed it somehow. Those bright slipcovers and the fresh flowers make all the difference. You've always loved flowers, haven't you?" She went to the window to look out. There was nothing to see, of course, but the high, impersonal buildings across the street and the constant flow of traffic below. She drifted around, looking at books, at the illustrations clipped to the drawing board, too restless to sit down. When I put the portfolio on my desk with a snap, she leaped as though a gun had gone off in her ear.

I went into the kitchen to make coffee, taking my time, giving her an opportunity to pull herself together, knowing how she hated to lose control. Then I added a jigger of rum to her cup and, on second thought, to my own, and carried the tray into the living room. Hope was standing before the fireplace looking down into the empty grate.

"No fires," I assured her cheerfully, and again she started at the sound of my voice. I pushed her into a chair and gave her the coffee. "Drink that before you try to talk."

So we drank coffee and, somewhat to my surprise, she let me refill her cup, again adding a jigger of rum. She began to talk then, idly. She asked me how I liked my apartment, how Winnie was getting along, and whether we saw much of each other.

"She seems to be excited about her job," I said.

"Excited?" Hope raised surprised brows and I noticed how deeply her eyes were shadowed.

"She said she had had no idea of what goes on in business. It's been a revelation, I take it."

"And it's safe to say she has overlooked nothing that came in her way," Hope commented. "Dad should never have inflicted her on a friend of his. He found out what she was like. He caught her prowling around the apartment more than once."

"Oh, surely not!" I protested.

Hope's lips curved in her faint, ironical smile. "In some ways you are unbelievably gullible. Winnie isn't just a tiresome person with the vice of prying. She's a —she tries to get a stranglehold. I didn't want her here, I can tell you that. She practically blackmailed me into giving her an apartment." After a pause Hope asked

39

whether I would mind if she turned over the vacant first-floor apartment to Hart Adams.

"Mind?"

"Well, he was Dad's closest associate, you know, and now there seems to be nothing left. The poor fellow is out of a job and he probably never saved much. I guess all of us assumed that he would be with Dad as long as they both lived." She made a grimace as though to keep herself from crying. "We thought that wouldn't be for years and years. I know how Dad felt about Hart, almost as though he were his own son. He wanted me to marry Hart. That's why he was so upset when I got engaged to Larry. He knew if I married Hart he would never go away. But Dad wanted me to be happy, so then he gave me the art gallery."

"Gave it to you?"

"To make sure that Larry would stay, you know," Hope said so naturally that I was silenced. *Like father, like daughter.* "Well, what with one thing and another, it would be better if Hart didn't stay at the apartment any longer. Anyhow, I'll probably have to sell it. So I thought it might suit him to live here, at least until he can get settled at some other job. He might have some difficulty, you know. Dad was the only person he had ever worked for and they say—now they say—"

"Personally," I said as though nothing was at stake beyond acquiring an agreeable neighbor, "I'd be delighted to have Hart here, and if I know Winnie, she'll set up loud cheers. There hasn't been a man within call until the agency sent us a superintendent a week ago."

"He's all right, isn't he?" Hope said anxiously. "The agent told me that we should have a man on the premises and that this one was reliable. His name is Maxwell Higgins and he is studying law at night and he needs a place to live. He's willing to look after the building, the furnace, the trash disposal, the general maintenance, in exchange for the basement room and a small salary. At least he is cheap, and that counts nowadays."

"So far as I know, he's fine. I haven't talked to him, but the place is a lot warmer since he came."

"That's good," Hope said vaguely, and I knew that she had already lost interest. Then she smiled at me. "It's heaven to see you, Sue. Always the same. Always dependable. The one human being I can really trust."

"Oh, surely not!" I said, shocked. Was this what the exposure of her father's criminal activities had done to her? But what had happened to her love for Larry, her faith in him?

Her face puckered like a small child's. "It's been awful. You have no idea. A nightmare that just goes on and on. The police got an anonymous letter saying that Dad had been murdered. You've heard that?"

I nodded. "Yes, but of course it's absurd. If there had been any question they would not have permitted —that is, the services would have been postponed, you know."

"There are different ways of killing people. Sue, they aren't telling me what they think, but I know they suspect that something brought about that heart attack, some shock, and they think, I know they think—Larry."

"No!" The cry tore from my throat before I could check it and then, in that revealing moment, Hope and I looked at each other, helpless in the face of my own betrayal. I tried to speak more quietly. "But that's fantastic. It's just plain impossible."

"Is it, Sue?" Hope asked gently.

II

Of course it was fantastic. I kept repeating that to myself all the rest of the afternoon. Larry a murderer? Ridiculous. There could be no conceivable reason for a man of Larry's character to turn to violence. But he had, I recalled, hated Marshall Phelps's guts because he believed, correctly as it turned out, that his hand, in a sense, had been the one that had held a gun to Graham Woods's head and destroyed a useful life. But you don't kill for a reason like that, not if you are a normal civilized human being. The eye-for-an-eye principle belongs to savagery.

Whether or not he approved of his father-in-law, Larry must have been grateful for his generosity, for a life of luxury in that beautiful apartment, for the art gallery. But Larry had been happy in his job of teaching. He hadn't wanted anything more than his shabby studio in the loft of an old factory building. He didn't gather moss.

My thoughts went round and round. Eventually I persuaded myself that the whole thing was nonsense, that Hope had endured so great a strain she was not thinking clearly. But had she fallen out of love with Larry? Had she lost faith in him? I remembered Winnie spitefully informing Hope that she had seen Larry with "a gorgeous blonde." Would Hope, knowing Winnie, have taken that seriously? She was so reserved that, except for the night when she had told me about her death sentence, I had never really known what she was thinking.

Late that afternoon there was a tap at the door and a sandy-haired young man, wearing jeans and a red flannel shirt, answered my call of "Come in." I could think better with a pencil in my hand and I was at the drawing board, sketching idly, while I tried to bring order out of turmoil.

"Miss Lockwood?" He had a pleasant voice. "I am Maxwell Higgins, the superintendent." He smiled at me. "I'm new to this and I want to make good. I just came up to say that you will find me on call at any time, day or night, and I hope you'll let me know if there's anything you don't like, or," and he glanced around the room, "any repairs. I'm not such a hot handyman, but I can do the usual things. I suppose you know where your fuse box is and things like that, just in case of emergency."

"As a matter of fact, I don't."

"Mind if I look around? Just as well to be familiar with the premises."

"Help yourself." I waved my hand and went back

to the drawing board. Under my fingers Winnie's face took shape. I wondered why Hope had seemed to imply that Winnie and I did not get along. It was true, of course, that there was a growing and very silent mutual dislike, but nothing that should have been apparent to anyone else.

Almost unconsciously I followed the progress of the young superintendent as he went from room to room: kitchen, bathroom, bedroom. He was thorough, if nothing else. I did not hear his return to the living room until he spoke behind me and then I leaped the way Hope had done earlier in the day.

"Sorry," he apologized. "I thought you heard me. I'm the original bull in the china shop." He looked at the sketch growing under my pencil. "That's the tenant upstairs, isn't it?" He hesitated. "Miss—"

"Winston," I told him.

He grinned spontaneously. "I don't figure I'd show that to her."

I realized that I had emphasized the pursed mouth, the malice in her smile, the avidity in her eyes. I ripped the sketch off the board and crumpled it to toss into the wastebasket. "Just an exercise."

He grinned again, not an impertinent grin but one with a kind of friendly complicity, and I found myself smiling back at him.

He glanced at the record player on which I had the Bach *Goldberg Variations* and laughed. "A friend of my aunt's dropped in to inspect my bachelor's quarters one day when I was playing that and she said, 'Oh, I just love Goldberg!' " I joined in his laughter.

"Well, I didn't mean to take up your time. Just to say that I'm around and to give you my phone number if you should want to call me, and all that."

"You are studying law, I understand."

He was surprised. "Yes, but how did you know?"

"Mrs. Garland told me. She owns this building, you know. She mentioned you when she dropped in this afternoon."

"The pretty woman in mourning?"

I nodded. "She's an old friend; she and Miss Winston who has the apartment above mine and I used to be known in college as The Inseparables."

He looked, as though unconsciously, at the drawing board on which I had been sketching that unflattering picture of Winnie but, aside from a twitch at the corners of his mouth, he made no sign.

"Well—oh, by the way, I found your fuse box. It's in the kitchen in that cabinet under the sink."

"Thank you." I waited for him to leave.

He turned back from the door. Apparently, like adolescents, he thought he had gone when he had said good-bye. "Have you been troubled by peddlers in the building, prowlers, anything like that?"

"So far as I know, there has never been anyone." I knocked on wood.

His glance sharpened. "And your friend, Miss Winston?"

"She has an office job and she's away all day. If anyone had bothered her at night, I'm sure she would have mentioned it."

He nodded, opened the door, and hesitated. "The top floor is supposed to be unoccupied, isn't it?"

"Supposed to be? It's been vacant ever since I moved in."

This time he really went out, closing the door behind him.

That night Winnie stopped on her way home. She came in with her usual sharp look of curiosity that took in the fresh flowers on my desk and the slack suit I was wearing. It was a plum-colored flannel tailored magically and as becoming as anything I had ever worn, though I was better-dressed these days because the chief perquisite of my modeling job was getting clothes at wholesale.

Winnie pulled off the small fur hat she had bought to match Hope's fur coat and ran a hand through her hair. She looked tired and, unexpectedly, worried.

"It must have been a tough day," I commented.

"I've had better. My boss came in while I was doing

some filing this afternoon and raised hell because I was going through some personal files. How was I supposed to know they were sacred cows or something?" She looked aggrieved, but I thought she was rather frightened too, and I remembered Larry saying once that someday her curiosity would get her into trouble. I was still too prone to remember the things Larry had said.

"Here, give me that coat. You'll swelter. Anyhow, there's snow on it. I'll hang it in the bathroom. How about a drink?"

"I could certainly use one," she admitted.

"Martini all right?"

"If there isn't anything else. I'd rather have Scotch."

So I prepared highballs. When I came back, she was, as I might have expected, looking through the sketches on the drawing board and I was glad I'd thrown away the unkind one of her. I served the drinks and said, "Skoal."

"Cheers." She lifted her glass and took three long swallows before she set it down. "That's a good-looking outfit, Sue. You must be making money hand over fist." She had never succeeded in learning just how much I did make and the fact tormented her.

"Probably a third of what you do. I got this wholesale. By the way, Hope was here this afternoon."

Winnie sat upright. "She was! That's odd, isn't it?"

"Not so odd, considering not only that I'm an old friend of hers but that she owns this building."

"What did she want?"

"She didn't want anything." I could hear the sharpness in my voice. "Not for herself, anyhow. She wants to give that first-floor apartment to Hart, who is out of a job now, you know."

"So she's putting him out of the Fifth Avenue apartment. Or," and Winnie's eyes were bright, "I sort of wonder, do you suppose Larry got fed up with Hart making sheep's eyes at Hope all the time and kicked him out as soon as his father-in-law died?"

I sipped my drink and made no reply, carefully made

no reply. After brooding for a minute Winnie said, "I've been thinking for a long time there was something wrong with that ménage, though I must say, whatever happened, I'll be glad to have Hart here."

"I thought you didn't like him," I said in some surprise. "You're always rather—disparaging when you speak of him."

"Heavens, no one could dislike Hart. No, but I'm glad to have any man in this place." When I laughed, she said, "I suppose you can't hear it from here."

"Hear what?"

"Footsteps. Someone moving around on the fourth floor." Seeing my obvious disbelief, she said, "Not often, just once in a while. It's probably a tramp who found the place was unoccupied, or maybe," and she shivered as the idea struck her, "someone comes there to that empty apartment for some—evil purpose."

"You sound like *The Mysteries of Udolpho*," I told her.

"Maybe. Just the same I've had a chain and a bolt installed on my door and I think you should too."

"Better than that, we've finally got a superintendent. He seems to be eager to help us, as he wants to keep the job. Here's his phone number in case you need him, or," I added, "next time you hear someone prowling around the fourth floor at night."

"Very funny," she said sourly.

I smiled and then the smile faded as I recalled the superintendent inquiring about the fourth floor and prowlers in the building. Perhaps I had better ask him to investigate or have him put a new lock on the door in the unlikely case that anyone was actually getting in, though what anyone would want in an uninhabited and unfurnished apartment, I could not imagine.

I didn't say anything about this to Winnie. She was tired and uncharacteristically upset, probably because of her clash with her employer, and there was no point in making her more nervous.

I had eaten a baked potato and some creamed chipped beef, not much of a meal, but I hated eating alone and usually did what was easiest. I had cleared up the kitchen, looked at the *TV Guide,* which as usual was unpromising, and picked up *Pride and Prejudice,* for perhaps the twentieth time, when I heard the familiar tap at the door and went to admit Roger Mullen.

He thrust a bunch of chrysanthemums into my hands and looked appreciatively at the slack suit. "Very nice," he declared. "Very, very nice."

When I had come back with a tall vase for the flowers, which I set on the floor beside the empty grate, I found him sprawled in an easy chair, looking disparagingly at Miss Austen's enchanting novel.

"High time I came to set your life on a different course. And that's what I am about to do, lady. The future is opening up to one of those technicolor finishes with two handsome profiles silhouetted against a glowing sunset. Here it is. Brace yourself. When we finish work on the present opus, I want to do a book on the Scandinavian countries. I haven't been there in three years and things change. How about coming along on this one? We could leave here in February or early in March and take six months, seeing all the byways as well as the highways. How does that strike you?"

"It sounds wonderful," I admitted. To go away, far away, to escape from Hope's tragedy and the terrifying suggestion that Larry might have committed a murder, to escape from my own heartache and emptiness. Wonderful, indeed.

"The simplest thing," he said with elaborate carelessness, "would be for us to get married first. Save a lot of complications. Anyhow it would be cheaper, one room instead of two."

I laughed. "Never have I heard a more romantic proposal."

He looked at me in silence and then prowled around the room in an aimless manner. Finally he went out to the kitchen, where I heard him emptying an ice tray and mixing drinks. He brought back two glasses. I saw the color of mine.

"For heaven's sake! What is this?"

"Just the first step toward what Bennett Cerf called a little whisky and sofa."

He moved over to sit beside me on the couch, and for once he was not laughing, he was deadly serious. He took my glass away from me and set it, with his own, on the table, and put his arms around me. "Don't be foolish, girl. You know I'm crazy about you. I'm the man you need in your life. We can make something special of it, combining our work and our pleasure and—" His arms tightened and he kissed me, not as he usually did, but a demanding kiss. He reached out to switch off the lamp and lifted his mouth from mine to say thickly, "There is a tide in the affairs of men—"

I was unhappy and frightened. Roger was gentle but insistent.

"I'm going to make love to you," he said.

I turned my mouth to meet his kiss. And the telephone rang.

"Don't go," he whispered. "Don't go."

But the ringing went on and on. I pushed him away and groped my way through the dark room to answer the phone and silence that determined ringing.

"Is this Mrs. Waldon?" asked a strange voice.

"Wrong number," I said rather breathlessly. Then, my sanity returning, I pulled myself together and went to switch on the light. I smiled at Roger and shook my head. "Wrong number," I told him. He did not insist. He too knew that the moment had passed.

Chapter 4

Evidently Hope had asked me about having Hart take the first-floor apartment merely as a gesture of courtesy, because the next day moving men appeared and all morning there was a cold draft on my feet from the open door downstairs as they trudged back and forth, installing a kitchen range and refrigerator, which required a great deal of thumping and grunting, and calling back and forth as they were moved into place and plugged in. From my bedroom I could hear furniture being put in the room below and a crash as a window was flung open on the fire escape which ran its unsightly way from the first floor to the roof.

When I had to go out on my modeling job, I edged my way around a man balancing on his shoulders a rolled carpet and another carrying bedsprings. By the time I got home that night, the door of the first-floor apartment was open and Hart, in shirt sleeves, was unpacking a valise. He turned swiftly and called, "Hello, there! Come on in."

"Just a moment to say welcome," I told him. "How did you get all this done so quickly?"

"Hope," he said, in the special tone he kept for her. "She arranged about the apartment and the furniture, had a telephone installed, and she even sent a woman along this afternoon to make the bed and get out towels and things."

The apartments, of course, were all alike; at least the shells were. Winnie's was so cluttered with furniture that it was difficult to move without bumping into things. Evidently she had been unable to refuse anything she could cram in. As her furniture was upholstered in dark green and there were heavy green draperies at the windows and a green carpet on the floor, the effect was gloomy. My own apartment was light and bright and gay, with color to compensate for the small amount of daylight that can filter down through New York's canyons. Hart's was simply a furnished apartment, impersonal, colorless, with Venetian blinds at the windows because there is no privacy on the first floor, especially at night with the lights on.

Hart held out his hand, looked at his grimy paw, and laughed. "Look, Sue, I haven't had a chance to put in any food yet and anyhow I'm a lousy cook. Won't you help me celebrate this housewarming," and I thought there was a wry twist to his mouth, "by having dinner with me?"

I was not anxious for another encounter with Roger until I had regained my equilibrium and decided what I was going to do—because there could be no more drifting now—so I accepted promptly.

"Would you like to come up for a drink first?"

"As soon as I can put away these clothes and get cleaned up." Hart glanced at the three suitcases on the floor. "What did you do with your luggage? Is there a storeroom here?"

"I borrowed a couple of suitcases from Hope when I moved in and then returned them to her. I don't know about storage space. You might ask the superintendent."

"That's an idea. He's already been up, taking a look at the stuff coming in. Seems to be the careful type."

By the time Hart came up, I had changed to a soft leaf-green wool dress whose subtle lines were already making it a fashion craze, and I had set out the makings for drinks, highball or cocktail, whichever he might prefer, and a small silver ice tub that Hope had given me when I moved in.

As I had expected, Roger telephoned, but I told him I had another engagement for dinner. He accepted my refusal with his usual sweetness of temper. "Just don't let the guy get any ideas," he said, and he gave a villain's laugh.

"He won't."

"And don't forget the cocktail party we are going to tomorrow." Jenkins, who published Roger's books, was giving a party to celebrate the publication of a new and brilliant biography of Gauguin, one which discarded most of the clichés of the past and the romanticized version created by Somerset Maugham. It had been selected by the Book of the Month Club and was off to a flying start. All the available authors in the Jenkins stable were expected to attend, as well as some prominent art critics and, of course, the media.

"Remember that some of this is to be used on TV," Roger warned me. "Wear your best bib and tucker and do me proud."

I was smiling when I returned to find Hart busy mixing the drinks. "Yours is a martini," he said. "I remember, you see. Gin or vodka?"

"Gin." As he hesitated, I said, "I don't really care, whichever you prefer."

"I got the vodka habit when I was with Mr. Phelps," he said. "It covers a multitude of sins, you know, like the cocktail before lunch and the extra nightcap."

I was surprised. "I did not know that Mr. Phelps ever made personal demands."

"Not of his guests, of course, but an employee—" He poured the cocktails and handed one to me. "I like this place of yours, Sue." His pleasant face looked rather tired and drawn, but whether from the nuisance of moving or the strain of the past weeks, I did not know. "Are you happy here?" he asked abruptly.

"Well—"

He nodded. "That was a stupid question, of course, but are you—well, contented?"

"Why not? The apartment could not be more conveniently located for my job, the modeling I do." I broke off. "You know, Hart, it just occurred to me that Hope will probably have to sell this house now. Apparently there isn't anything left."

51

"Her father wanted her to hang onto it for a while at least. They'll be starting to tear down the building to the east of it in a few days, which will probably be noisy as hell, and the pressure to sell will get stronger all the time."

"I suppose so."

"Do you see much of Hope?" he asked abruptly.

"Very little. Yesterday was the first time I have talked to her since before she was married."

"Yesterday?"

"She came down to see me and tell me that you'd be taking an apartment here. Apparently she is going to sell the Fifth Avenue apartment."

"Well, there is just no money to maintain it. God, Sue, I can't understand it! I never will understand it. He seemed—he was the finest—he had an upright—" Hart ran his fingers through his short-cut hair.

"And you never guessed?"

"How could I?" he asked simply.

I wanted to say, "How could you not?" but I refrained. Knowing his hero worship, I suppose it was possible for him to be blind to Phelps's real activities.

"Everything was on the up and up," he persisted. "The men he associated with—nothing wrong with them. Prominent men, most of them. Everything I handled was as clean as a whistle."

And that, it occurred to me, was probably true. There could not conceivably be a better cover for a man than this assistant who was so incorruptible and so blatantly honest.

"But there must be something left," I persisted. "There has to be money somewhere, some assets."

"The Fifth Avenue apartment, this house, and the art gallery. But both the house and the art gallery belong to Hope. Phelps's creditors can't touch them, of course."

"I suppose she will sell the gallery now. That ought to bring in something and Larry could go back to teaching. He always loved that."

"Larry? Oh, that's right, you knew him before Hope married him."

I made no comment, but held out my empty glass for a refill.

When Hart came back, he said, "I've always wondered about Garland. I know Hope fell for him in college and he married her in a rush. I suppose he knew he wasn't apt to meet that much money again. And she's so—vulnerable, you know. There must be a kind of animal magnetism a man like that has. He even managed to get around Mr. Phelps, which was quite a feat, because Phelps didn't want Hope to marry him. But the two of them, father and daughter, were almost a closed corporation. I'm surprised there was even room in it for Garland. But these last few weeks I sort of wondered—there was a kind of tension—" Hart's voice trailed off and then he said, "Have you ever seen the gallery? It has some terrific stuff and Garland seems to be doing well with it. And, of course, when the market is uncertain, as it is now, people buy paintings because they consider them a safer investment than stocks."

"No, I haven't seen it."

"Oh, I wondered." He added awkwardly, "I knew there was some girl, some stunning girl, he seems to be seeing. So I wondered."

"He hasn't been seeing me," I told him dryly, and after a quick glance he dropped the subject.

We were on our way out to dinner and I was locking the door when Winnie came out of her apartment. She paused halfway down the flight, eyes bright. "Well, hello there," she said, giving the words so much emphasis that anyone might have supposed that Hart and I had been detected in some unseemly posture. She gave a coy laugh. "Cheering the bachelor's lonely evening?"

Hart gave me a quick, amused glance. "That's it," he said. He looked at me. "Luchow's or would you rather go somewhere closer at hand? Pronounce, I am tame."

"We'd never get a table at Luchow's in Christmas week without a reservation."

Winnie, as usual, stumbled over the hole in the stair carpet.

"Chez Louis be all right?"

"Fine."

"Well, of all the coincidences," Winnie exclaimed unconvincingly, "that's where I was going. Maybe we can share a cab."

Hart gave me a dismayed look and then accepted defeat like a scholar and a gentleman. "Delighted to have you with us," he said.

The dinner was superb, I suppose, but by the time it was over, I thought Winnie's insistent questions were going to drive Hart up the wall. Right up to the coffee stage he managed to keep a tight rein on his irritation, and then it slipped.

"For God's sake, Winnie, cut it out! For weeks I've spent most of my time, day and night, answering questions. I'm fed to the teeth."

"I can imagine. What did they ask you, Hart?"

"One more question and I'm going to gag you, Winnie," I warned her. "Come on. Hart has just moved and he's tired. Let's go home."

She yielded reluctantly but because she had no alternative. As she clung like a limpet, Hart stopped at his own door to say good night and Winnie and I went up together. Winnie's last comment was typical of her. "Just think, it's almost Christmas. I guess Hope isn't going to invite us this year. It will be sort of strange, having Christmas all alone, but I don't suppose she'll feel like entertaining, though it isn't as though we were outsiders. I think she might have asked us."

"No," Hart said harshly, "she doesn't feel like entertaining," and his tone silenced Winnie.

At my door Winnie paused. "Well, so now you're going to have another beau."

"Considering that Hart has never looked at any girl in his life except Hope, aren't you being rather ridiculous?"

"Just the same, it is always a good idea to let a man know he has competition, isn't it?"

"What man?"

"The one who is always coming to see you. I think you said you were working together."

"I probably said it because it's true. I'm illustrating a travel book he has written."

"Oh. Well, I guess I'll have to talk with that new superintendent. I like to know about people who are in the same building. I feel safer that way, don't you?"

"I hadn't thought about it." I opened my door and went in. I heard Winnie going slowly up the stairs as though somehow she had been cheated of some treat she expected.

II

As usual the store windows were filled with Christmas displays, there was a Santa Claus on every corner ringing his bell, shoppers thronged Fifth Avenue and Thirty-fourth Street, Twenty-third and Fourteenth, attracted by some fascinating display, plodding on tired feet, looking for bargains, or caught up in the general excitement. There were carolers at Rockefeller Center and skaters on the frozen rink, moving to canned music. The giant tree soared above them with its Christmas decorations.

For once I had no heart for Christmas jollifications and I did not attempt to decorate my apartment. I was in no mood for a Christmas party when Roger called for me. My only concession to the season a sprig of holly pinned to my coat.

He looked at me and whistled. "You are really going to be the star attraction." He leaned over to kiss me lightly on the cheek, his own lips cold. It was a bitter day, frostily clear but with a biting wind.

He turned me so I could see myself in the long mirror I had hung over the fireplace, tilted so that I got a view of the couple standing there, Roger with his cheeks reddened by cold, his eyes smiling as he looked at me, and me in a red suit I had modeled the week before.

It was simple but with the kind of lines only an inspired dressmaker can design. Roger put over my shoulders the black dyed muskrat coat I had bought at a sale earlier in the season, with a fur-lined hood that was, if I do say so, madly becoming.

Roger had a cab waiting at the door and gave the address of the St. Moritz. "Jenkins is really going to town," I remarked.

"With the book-club deal he can afford it. Oh, and by the way, I caught him in a weak moment and he's all steamed up about that Scandinavian project." Roger made no further comment and I said nothing, holding my coat tight around my throat as we crossed the windswept sidewalk and entered the warm lobby.

"Roof," Roger told the elevator operator and I saw the group of people crowding in with us. Apparently this was going to be one of those Standing Room Only affairs, with every available celebrity drawn into the net.

And it was all that. At one end of the room there was a bar. At the other a small orchestra played softly. Little tables were scattered around and the guests, already a mob, were circulating, stopping to chat, helping themselves to hors d'oeuvres and drinks from the trays carried by waiters.

Photographers were busy snapping the guests, and I remembered that part of this affair was to be televised. A knowledgeable reporter was murmuring the names of the guests to a photographer, indicating the most prominent people.

Roger and I approached the publisher and his star author, who turned out to be an unexpectedly young man to have written so brilliant and scholarly a book. A photographer snapped me and I found myself responding with the professional smile I wore like a mask when I was modeling. This, at least, I was accustomed to.

We stopped to speak to Jenkins and to the author who said, "Who? Susan Lockwood? And you often come in and out of the office? Why," he demanded indignantly, "have I never met you before?"

"We're stopping traffic, Sue," Roger said, and started to lead me toward a group of cronies with whom he had exchanged waves, when I stopped short. The tall, rangy man entering the big room was Larry. He paused for a moment, seeking out his host, and his eyes caught mine. For a moment we stood staring at each other. Because neither of us had expected the encounter, we were unprepared, stripped of our defenses. We had each taken an involuntary step toward the other when we were startled to hear the publisher exclaim, "Oh, here is Dr. Garland. This is our guest of honor, Clayton Baxter. I know you two will have a lot in common. I see they are beginning to get set up for your little talk and I understand you both preferred it to be unrehearsed. Shall we move over there? Ready, gentlemen?"

There was a bustle as efficient technicians posted the two men against a neutral backdrop, arranged lights, and seated them in chairs that revolved so that they could sit at ease and without rigid self-consciousness. There was a hush in the room and the waiters had stopped moving about. Then I heard the muted voice of a well-known interviewer introduce the two men, and Larry said, in the easy, relaxed manner he had used in the seminar—why on earth had I thought he would be nervous?—"I don't need to tell you that you've done a wonderful job, Mr. Baxter. What attracted you to Gauguin as a subject?"

"I don't know why one subject attracts a writer irresistibly. This one certainly attracted me and yet I didn't like Gauguin as a man and I'm not completely sold on him as a painter."

"And yet you have managed to bring out factors that escaped the experts. Can you—"

They talked for perhaps five minutes. Then there was a general bustle, the photographers and sound men moved away, the two men stood up, shook hands, and the publisher instantly cornered his guest and began to introduce him to the clamoring public.

At last, though he had not glanced at me a second time, but as though he had known that I would be waiting, Larry turned to me. He looked at my suit and at Roger, who was holding my arm in a proprietary way as he prepared to steer me through the crowd to his friends. It was like coming face to face with a total stranger.

"Well, Sue, you seem to be flourishing."

"And you, Larry. That's a nice job you did for our prize author."

"Our author?"

"I'm in this stable too, though just a minor figure, of course. And this is Roger Mullen, who is not a minor figure. You must know his offbeat travel books. Dr. Garland, Roger."

"You knew how to bring out all the most telling points, Dr. Garland," Roger said. "Very impressive job." He looked from me to Larry. "You'll want to catch up on old times, Sue. See you over at the table in the corner," and he drifted away.

"Quite the little gent, isn't he?" Larry said. "Your newest conquest?"

I was torn between the impulse to hit him and a desire to burst into tears. And I stood there, unable to speak, but, instinctively, as the photographers began to circulate among the people again, I turned slightly because at full face the figure is badly displayed and it had become second nature to pose. Larry noticed it. He grinned sardonically. "You seem to have learned all the tricks of the celebrity."

"Not a celebrity," I said evenly, "a model. That's how I earn my living. Didn't you know?"

"A model!" His jaw dropped ludicrously.

"How did you think I earned my living? I model clothes for a department store and on the side I do illustrating."

"I see." He stood looking at me blankly, at a loss for words.

I had control of myself now. "So nice to have seen you," I said brightly, and turned away.

His hand shot out and caught my wrist. "Wait, Sue!" He managed a smile. "This calls for a drink," and he signaled a waiter.

"Why does it?"

"Well, as your friend said, we've got to catch up on old times."

"Oh!" I choked and turned blindly away. "I must go."

"Not yet. I've got to talk to you. There are a lot of things we've got to clear up."

"No," I said sharply.

His hand tightened on my wrist, then he released it and took two glasses from the tray, handing one to me. "Still martinis?"

"Still. I haven't changed that much," and I broke off. This was hell. I had to get away.

Then Larry was smiling easily, any pleasant guest at any party. "I thought the commentator was very tactful, didn't you? A nice buildup for the gallery and not a word about my defunct father-in-law."

Something in his tone startled me. "You never really forgave him, did you, Larry?"

"I hated his guts."

I put out my hand in protest, clutched his sleeve. "Larry, don't say that! Don't let anyone else hear you say that, for heaven's sake!"

There was a queer expression on his face. "So you've been hearing rumors, have you? My, my, how these things get around! Where did you get that little morsel?"

I could not tell him that it was from Hope. I simply looked at him and his eyes narrowed in speculation. He had always been quick to read my thoughts and I did not want him to do so now.

"You said—anyone else? Does that mean you believe I did not murder my father-in-law?"

"I—of course not! I said it was ridic—" I broke off. "Give my love to Hope." I placed my untouched glass on the tray of a passing waiter and went quickly across the room to join Roger and his friends. I thought Roger

59

looked at me rather soberly as he rose to introduce me to the little group of men, but I must have been mistaken, as we were soon engaged in lighthearted talk, laughter rising like smoke from the table and reaching Larry, who stood where I had left him, still looking at me.

He knows it was Hope who told me, I thought miserably.

After the cocktail party Roger and I were gathered up in a group that seemed to be growing like a snowball and we all ended by having dinner at a Chinese restaurant.

On the ride home Roger did not mention Larry. He was quiet until we reached the house. Then he said, "Will you spend Christmas with me, Sue?" Before I could protest, he said, "I know you aren't in a holiday mood, but two can do better than one. And if you prefer Galahads to men—and personally I don't think you know what you want at this moment—I'll be the original knight in armor. Fair enough?"

"Thank you, Roger. I'd like that. You are really very sweet."

"And that," he said grimly, holding my arm so I would not slip on the snow, "is the unkindest cut of all. What I need is a brand-new image." He kissed me lightly, said, "Thanks for letting me squire the loveliest woman in the place. It helps build my ego," and he went back to get in the cab.

I was so preoccupied that, like Winnie, I stumbled over the hole in the stair carpet and nearly fell down.

Before going to bed, I mixed a drink and then poured it down the sink and heated a glass of milk instead. What I wanted was not stimulation but sleep. Restlessly I switched on the television for the eleven o'clock news, saw the usual battle scenes in countries ostensibly at peace, got the usual report of the revelations of corporate and governmental dishonor that had an odd sound at this holiday season, saw the sports, and then, under the heading of "People in the News," saw the cocktail party given for our author, saw the celebrities, saw Larry discussing the book with its author, and then saw Larry and me, staring at each other like people bemused, his hand on my wrist. It was a dead giveaway. I could feel color burn in my cheeks, on my forehead, on my throat. My whole body seemed to be one blush. On television. Oh, God! On television.

I shut off the set, stumbled into my room and then was called back by the strident ringing of the telephone.

"Sue? This is Hope. Is Larry there?"

"Is Larry—what!"

"So he isn't. All right, I'll buy that. You never could lie convincingly. He hasn't come home and I thought— I just saw the two of you in the news, looking at each other as though you were Romeo and Juliet."

"I've never seen him since that day at college, Hope. I didn't expect to see him today. That is the absolute truth. If I had known he was going to be at the cocktail party, I'd have stayed away."

"Come to see me tomorrow, will you? It's important, Sue, or I wouldn't ask. Come about three, if you can possibly manage it. I've simply got to talk to you." She added, "Larry won't be here then."

Chapter 5

So at three o'clock on December the twenty-third I found myself getting out of the elevator at the Fifth Avenue apartment. There were two doors in the little corridor: one led to what had been Marshall Phelps's library, the other stood open and a uniformed maid was waiting for me.

"Good afternoon, Frances."

"Good afternoon, ma'am. It's a long time since we've seen you. Mrs. Garland is in her morning room upstairs." She led the way through the big beautiful living room. One of the famous features of the apartment was the circular staircase that wound up out of the drawing room onto a balcony. Hope's suite was at the end of the hall and the maid, after tapping at the door, opened it for me and discreetly closed it behind me.

Hope, wearing an exquisite white velvet robe, was lying on a chaise longue, a soft white blanket over her knees.

She was pale, even her lips were colorless. She made a little gesture toward a chair. "This was good of you, Sue. Do sit down. I won't keep you long."

Something in her tone took me aback. After an intimate friendship of four years, she was treating me with the gracious detachment she might have used toward an employee who had come at her summons. For a moment I was tempted to turn around and go out but, seeing her pallor, I could not do it.

"You're looking very prosperous," she said at last. I glanced around the familiar room and saw my sketch of Larry on the little table beside the chaise longue, which also held a carafe of water, a handkerchief, a small medicine bottle, a book and an odd-shaped cigarette case. There was also a brooch in the shape of a horseshoe, whose diamonds reflected red and green and yellow lights. Hope picked it up, turning it absently in her thin fingers. "My lucky piece. Dad gave it to me." She put it down with her little ironic smile. Her eyes came back to me, eyes that for once were calculating. "Last night I had a heart attack."

"Oh, Hope!"

"It's over now but I hadn't expected—and the doctor had not expected—I'd have such a bad one, not so soon." She raised herself a little on the chaise longue. "Sue, how could you do it to me?"

"If you mean Larry—"

"Of course I mean Larry."

"I told you the truth when you called last night. I've never seen him since the day I promised you I wouldn't. Not once. Yesterday I had to go to that cocktail party because my publisher expected his whole stable to be there, at least everyone within commuting distance of New York. I didn't even know Larry was invited. It was a chance encounter."

"You just spoke—and looked at each other—and parted."

"That's exactly what we did," I said levelly.

She was silent for a long time, her hands moving restlessly on the white blanket. "He didn't come home until nearly four this morning. He was drunk. I've never known him to be even high before. A couple of cocktails before dinner, once in a while a nightcap, and that's all." She was really angry. "In this building where everyone knows us! I've never been so humiliated."

I could feel a pulse beating wildly in my throat. I had been wrong about Larry. Perhaps he hated me; he had spoken as though he did, but that meeting had apparently shaken him as deeply as it had me if it had led him to get drunk.

"He wasn't with me, Hope. I had dinner with another man, actually a whole group that sort of accumulated at the party, and Roger brought me home before eleven."

"If you say so." Hope smiled faintly. "Perhaps I did you an injustice, Sue."

"You did all of us an injustice."

"All of us?"

"You and Larry and me. You should have known better than to work yourself into a heart attack about something that you must realize was untrue."

"You're really talking about Larry, aren't you? Well, the truth is that if he wasn't with you—all right, I'll accept the fact that he wasn't—then he was probably with his gorgeous blonde."

"For heaven's sake! I suppose that is part of the malicious nonsense Winnie told you. That girl is poison, Hope. She's envious of you. She fell for Larry herself, and she's envious of—all this," and I made a gesture indicating the room with its beautiful appointments. "If Larry ever did meet a gorgeous blonde, it was probably a cousin or an old pupil or—"

"Or." Again Hope smiled faintly. Then she nodded. "You may be right. I've learned for myself that Winnie is a rat. But things haven't been going well with Larry and me. Of course, after Dad—" She looked older when she referred to her father. "It has been unmitigated hell."

For the first time that afternoon she sounded like herself, the suspicion and hostility absent. "You can't have any idea, Sue. All the props knocked out from under me, all those revelations about Dad, when I had always thought he was so wonderful. And the questions. The questions!" Her head dropped back on the satin cushions. "And Larry changing. I don't understand it. I'm afraid. Terribly afraid. If it isn't because of you—why has he changed? What has gone wrong? What has he done?"

"I don't know," I said as calmly as I could. "Probably nothing. You're overwrought, Hope. You aren't getting things in perspective." I pushed back my chair. "I've got to go. There are some drawings I have to finish tonight." This wasn't true, but it served as well as any other excuse.

She pressed a button. "All right, Sue. It was kind of you to come. Only don't—" her voice broke— "don't ever fail me again, Sue."

"But I haven't—" I began when the door opened and the maid appeared.

"See Miss Lockwood out, will you, Frances? Goodbye, Sue. Merry Christmas."

I thought the maid looked at me rather curiously as she led the way down the circular staircase and across the great drawing room with its row of high windows facing Fifth Avenue and the Park. Other years a Christmas tree had stood beside the fireplace in which birch logs had been stacked, awaiting Christmas Eve. I was glad that Larry was not at home. It would have been unbearable to leave them together in this lovely room.

As the elevator door opened, Winnie got out. She had, I thought, been crying. She gave a startled gasp when she caught sight of me and almost scuttled past me toward the open door to the apartment where Frances was still standing.

II

On Christmas Eve I had no modeling to do and I had finished my work on Roger's book. I wandered around the apartment restlessly, unable to settle down to anything. It was the first time since my graduation that I had had no urgent job and there was little temptation to go out of doors if I could avoid it, because snow was falling heavily and a high wind blew it against the windowpane with a shushing sound and piled it on window ledges.

Only one thing was clear. I could no longer accept Hope's generosity and continue to live in her house. Her bitter accusation and suspicion made that impossible. I tried to pin my mind down to practical considerations, such as how much money I had on hand

and how much would be required to make a down payment on an apartment, because the landlord would probably demand at least two months in advance. Or perhaps I'd have to go back to a furnished room in the Village or the Bronx or Brooklyn.

A buzz of the bell indicated that the mailman had something too large to go in the box and I went down the stairs to sign for a large flat package, and to give the postman the envelope containing his Christmas tip. We were exchanging season's greetings when the outside door opened and Winnie came in, looking like a snowman. She seemed tired and worried and almost frightened but, being Winnie, her attention was caught at once by the package in my hand. I had already seen the return address and I turned it over hastily, but I felt, with a sinking of the heart, that I had been too late. Winnie had already seen it, which put the cap on what was already a completely miserable day.

She hovered tenaciously beside me until the postman had gone, while I busied myself in flipping over the heap of Christmas cards I had taken from my box.

"Did Hope send for you?" Winnie asked at last. "I wondered, when I saw the eleven o'clock news night before last, and there were you and Dr. Garland looking at each other that way. My dear!" There was malice in her smile. "Right on television! I can imagine Hope's fury. I'll bet she really lashed out. Did she threaten you, too?" Winnie tried to rectify that phrase. "I mean she seemed sort of beside herself, not her usual cool self at all. I'd never have thought she could be so downright venomous. And the things she said about Dr. Garland! Well, I always did think he was the world's worst heel."

"You were mad about him," I said, suddenly furious. "You still are. You've never forgiven Hope for marrying him."

"Well, I must say," Winnie began in an aggrieved voice. Hearing Hart open his door, I felt I could not endure much more and I ran upstairs to my own apartment.

The package, as I had seen at once, had the return

address of Larry's—Hope's?—art gallery. I had not known before that Larry ever worked in water colors. The picture was fairly large, perhaps fifteen inches by twenty-four. I was wearing a shabby sweater and skirt that I had had in college, and standing against a background of laurel in bloom. He must have painted it after that last afternoon we had had together. It was idealized, of course. I have never been beautiful and I have never had that kind of radiance in my face. Or had I on that one afternoon? If so, it had been a dead giveaway.

If I had wondered, now and then, about Larry's feeling for me, I knew the answer now. It was not over for him any more than it was for me. For a long time I looked at the picture until my eyes blurred. Then I put it gently in a drawer of my desk and, knowing Winnie, turned the key in the lock and then slid the key under the clock on the mantel above the empty grate.

In the hallway below I could hear Winnie and Hart talking, though I could not make out the words, and heaven knows I did not try. If there had been any doubt in my mind, I knew now that I had no choice about moving out of Hope's building. I must go at once.

Sometime later I answered a knock at the door, hoping it wouldn't be Winnie, and found a messenger with a package which, when I had admitted that I was Susan Lockwood, he put in my hands and accepted the fifty cents I gave him.

The package contained a little Christmas tree, not more than fifteen inches high, decorated with tinsel and artificial icicles, with cotton batting at the base and embedded in it a jeweler's box. I opened it and saw a ring set with a magnificent opal. There was a card in Roger's tiny writing:

> Will you wear this tomorrow? You're too special for diamonds. A Merry Christmas and a happy future for us both. Your Roger.

It was a beautiful ring, but I did not try it on. Somehow, knowing Roger, I was sure it would fit. The problem was that I did not know how far I wanted to be committed to Roger. I liked him immensely, I was fond of him; there were moments when my senses responded to him, whether or not my heart did. Or perhaps that did not matter. As Edna St. Vincent Millay had pointed out:

> Whether or not we find what we are seeking
> Is idle, biologically speaking.

He would be gentle and kind and understanding. We had a tremendous amount of interests in common. We would travel and work together and separately. Certainly it would be better to build a new life, starting now, at once, and if I married Roger, at least I would not have to start looking for another apartment. I could move into his charming apartment on Gramercy Park, where I had visited him several times.

I had all day and all night before I would see him and have to make up my mind whether to keep the ring or return it. But if I did return it, I realized with a pang, there could be no more happy work together. It wasn't fair that problems of earning a livelihood should interfere with personal problems, but somehow they had a way of doing so.

The superintendent followed a tap on the door by opening it. In honor of the holidays, perhaps, he wore a conventional gray business suit with a blue shirt and dark red tie. "I don't want to disturb you, Miss Lockwood, but I've been talking with Miss Winston, who complains about someone walking around in that fourth-floor apartment. Have you heard anyone?"

"Not a sound," I assured him. "I should warn you that Miss Winston has a tendency to imagine things."

"Oh, she didn't imagine this. Someone has been up there, all right. I could see the footprints in the dust."

"For heaven's sake! Why would anyone want to get

into a vacant apartment?" I was surprised to see how intently he was regarding me.

"That's got me puzzled too. I try to keep an eye on people coming and going. Anyone entering the house has to pass my window, you know. But, of course, I have to take care of the furnace, the garbage, and a lot of odds and ends. I can't look out of the window all the time."

"I don't much like the idea of someone getting in," I admitted. "Can't you put a new lock on the door, or something?"

"Not on Christmas Eve. Everything will be closed up by this time. But the day after Christmas I'll make sure the place is closed up as tight as a drum." He closed the door quietly behind him.

I switched on the television, got a sentimental Christmas story, and switched it off again. I tried the radio and got Christmas carols. If I heard anyone else sing "Joy to the World" I'd go up the wall. It was hard to bear all this synthetic gaiety when I was alone with nothing outside but the snow falling like a curtain and nothing inside but desolation.

In a mood of what I recognized as disgusting self-pity I went out to the kitchen to mix a couple of martinis. I went back, set the pitcher and a glass on the table beside the couch and looked over my records, seeking something to suit my mood. Not one of the last quartets, they cut too close to the bone. Not *Swan Lake* because I wasn't ready for facile prettiness. The *Sinfonia Concertante*. I settled back, a chilled glass in my hand, and listened to the lovely dialogue of violin and viola, as they spoke separately or joined together, linkèd sweetness long-drawn-out.

For a few minutes I was truly happy.

And then I heard the sound that had grown so familiar, a stumble as Winnie tripped over the hole in in the carpet on the stairs. Don't stop, I told her fiercely in my mind. Don't stop. Go away. I don't want to see you.

But no one came up the stairs. There was an odd

choking sound and then nothing. I waited for Winnie to pass my door. At length I stirred uneasily. After all, she might have fallen and hurt herself. I opened the door and peered down the stairs. As I did so, Hart's door opened. He looked up the stairs and then came running up as I ran down.

Winnie was unhurt. She was kneeling beside the crumpled body on the stairs, saying blankly, "She's dead. Hope is dead. Look—" She pointed a shaking finger at the throat in which a thin cord was imbedded. "Look!" She began to scream.

Chapter 6

After one look at Hope's distorted face I clutched at the railing to keep myself from falling. Hart had stopped now, shocked and horrified. And then Higgins, the superintendent, was there, his voice crisp.

"Don't touch anything," he said in a tone of authority, and Winnie's screaming broke off in a kind of gasp. I saw then that Hope's huge handbag had opened as she fell and the contents were spilled on the stairs. Winnie drew back her hand with a jerk as though she had burned it.

"Good God!" Hart was saying over and over. "Good God!" Then he shoved Winnie away and knelt beside Hope, his hands at her throat.

"Stop that!" Higgins said.

"But we've got to get it off!"

The superintendent eyed him curiously. "She is quite dead, Mr. Adams."

"Oh, no! Not Hope." Hart staggered against the wall and I remembered the years of his unswerving devotion.

"I'll call the police." My voice sounded strange in my ears, as hollow as though I were speaking in a cave.

"I've done so, Miss Lockwood. If you'll please get up, Miss Winston—no, don't touch anything."

"But that's Hope's gold compact. She wouldn't want it just lying there."

Higgins ignored her preposterous silliness. "Leave everything just as it is." He turned in relief as the door opened and two men in uniform came in. "The dead woman is Mrs. Lawrence Garland who owns this building but does not live here. She was found like this by Miss Winston—when?"

Winnie's lips opened and closed. "Just now."

One of the men from the patrol car leaned forward and touched Hope's cheek, her throat, her hand. "She's still warm."

Winnie gulped. "I was just coming in and there she was and I thought she'd fallen over that hole in the carpet—and I do think something should be done about that. It's an outrage the way things are neglected around here. Someone might be killed—" She broke off.

"You've just come in?" one of the policemen said rather oddly, and I noticed that her coat was dry, without a trace of snow.

"I'll call in," one of the men from the patrol car said and went out. The draft as the door closed made a lock of Hope's fair hair stir, lifting and falling as though she were alive. The other man took out a notebook. Before he could ask any questions, the superintendent opened his wallet and showed it to him. The policeman looked at it, looked at Higgins in surprise, and made a note. "I'll talk to you later. You live here?"

"I'm the superintendent. You'll find me in the basement apartment."

"You?" the policeman asked Winnie.

"Winifred Winston."

"Address?"

"I live here."

"Occupation?"

A moment's pause. "I have a clerical job with the construction firm of Rogers and Rogers."

"You knew this lady?"

"She was my best friend." Winnie began to cry.

"You had better go to your apartment," the policeman said. "Someone will question you later."

"But—"

"Now, please," he said, and she edged her way past the crumpled body and went up the stairs.

"You?"

"My name is Susan Lockwood and I have the second-floor apartment." I anticipated his next question. "Mrs. Garland was an old friend."

As I was going up, I heard him say, "Your name, please?"

"Hart Adams. I—" His voice broke and he steadied it. "I've known Mrs. Garland all her life. I was her father's secretary. He was Marshall Phelps."

"Phelps!" the word came out like an explosion. Then I heard the policeman say, "You'd better sit down somewhere."

"My apartment is on this floor."

"We'll find you there. Please don't leave the building until someone has talked to you." The policeman added sharply, "Please don't touch the body!"

"I just—to say good-bye. And someone ought to notify her husband."

"Here—you aren't going to faint, are you?"

"Of course not." There was a crash and I heard the policeman calling for Higgins, who came running up the stairs from the basement just as the front door opened and the other policeman came in.

"They're on their way," he said cheerfully. "Hey, for God's sake, we got another corpse?"

"Guy fainted. He took the lady's death hard."

I heard the confusion as the men lifted Hart and carried him into his apartment. The *Sinfonia Concertante* wove its serene and lovely way toward the end of the second movement and the record shut off with a snap. My knees were shaking and I collapsed on the couch, reached for my cocktail glass and refilled it. The glass rattled against my teeth as I held it with both hands, but a few sips helped to clear my head.

And at last I was able to think. Someone had put a noose around Hope's neck. She had died by violence within the past few minutes, within yards of where I had been listening to the Mozart. Died of violence. There had been no words. I would have been sure to hear if she had spoken to anyone, and Hope would surely have spoken to anyone she knew. It must, of course, be the work of our prowler.

For some time, because of the holiday, the end of the rush of Christmas shopping, and the heavy fall of snow, the street had been quiet, with practically no traffic. The heavy trucking was over and nothing was left but a few private cars and cruising taxis. Now there was the rumble of motors, the slamming of car doors, and the sound of voices. I went to the window. There were several police cars and a number of men piling out of them. One of the men from the patrol car came out of the building and I saw that he was speaking to the newcomers. Then there was an exclamation.

"Marshall Phelps's daughter! Then this is going to be a big one."

The cold draft swirled around my feet and I knew that the outside door had opened. After that there was confusion as large men maneuvered on the narrow stairs, examining the body that lay so still, the body with that unspeakably distorted and discolored face. The men who saw her now would never know how pretty Hope had been, I thought, in my first feeling of grief and loss.

The old-fashioned chandelier vibrated as it always did when Winnie walked in the living room upstairs. She had a heavy, flat-footed tread, and though the floor was carpeted, the vibration set the crystals in the chandelier to tinkling.

I found myself thinking about Winnie's coat. She had been indoors long enough for the snow to melt, so she was lying about that. But Winnie—no, that was too absurd. Apparently she had had a quarrel with Hope, but even if she was resentful, she would never have been driven to violence. She was as incapable of violence as I was. As Hart was. At least, where Hope had been concerned.

Feet tramped up and down the stairs, the place was noisy with voices, and all the time I was listening for the one voice that should be heard. Why didn't Larry come?

After a long time blinking lights attracted my attention and I went to the window as an ambulance drew up. After a few minutes a stretcher was carried out on which a small figure was carried, face as well as body covered by a blanket. The ambulance moved away quietly. There was no hurry about this trip.

And then, after what seemed to be hours, the cars began to leave, all except one. The police would be coming to question me now, but the halls were silent. Apparently they were taking the superintendent first.

It was dark, as dark as Manhattan ever gets at night with street lights and lights in the high buildings, and a white glow lighting the western sky from Broadway, even through the heavy fall of snow. Down the street a hotel was brightly lighted and I could hear a constant shrill whistle as the doorman signaled for cruising taxis.

Six o'clock. Seven. I walked the floor from window to door, from door to window. What on earth could the superintendent have to say that could keep them so long? And at last I heard the sound for which I had been listening. Two men were coming up the uncarpeted basement stairs. Instinctively I braced myself for the interview and then relaxed as there was a knock at Hart's door. Poor Hart. Poor Hart! The whole pattern of his life had been smashed by the hands that had tightened that noose around Hope's neck.

Eight o'clock. I realized that I was faint, not so much from shock as from lack of food. I could not face solid food, but I mixed an eggnog and drank it as I continued to pace the floor. And then I heard the heavy footsteps, but this time they went up to the fourth floor. Apparently the police took seriously the idea of a prowler. Well, what else? After all, it was the only possible explanation. Now they were coming down and they stopped at the third floor. I heard the firm knock and Winnie's voice quavering, "Who is it?"

"The police, ma'am."

When chain, bolt, and key had all been released, the chandelier vibrated as two men walked across Winnie's cluttered living room.

Nine o'clock. I had long since stopped pacing and when the knock came at my door, I was almost too tired to care. Neither of the men was in uniform, but no one would have mistaken their profession. They were both big and squarely built, with observant eyes. The older one was beginning to run to fat; he had a double chin and a bald spot over which he had carefully brushed a few hairs. He was Lieutenant Saxby. The other, with an odd-shaped face, narrow at the forehead and wide at the jaw, was Sergeant Clark. Until they stood looking around the room, I had forgotten that the martini glass was very much in evidence.

When I had found ashtrays for them and they were seated, the lieutenant began to talk in an easy, commonplace sort of way that made my tense muscles relax and I expelled a long breath. He smiled at me and nodded in approval. "That's better."

We went through what I supposed were the usual preliminaries: my name, age, occupation—the word model made them look up alertly and I explained that I modeled clothes. I also mentioned the book I had just finished illustrating.

"You knew the deceased?"

The deceased. That was Hope.

"Very well," I said huskily, and then went on more clearly. The two men were tired and probably hungry and undoubtedly they had been treated to a fine sample of Winnie's hysteria, but I tried to answer as succinctly as I could. "Mrs. Garland and Miss Winston and I were close friends all through college where we were known as The Inseparables."

"Then this comes to you as a personal loss as well as an emotional shock."

I nodded.

"Apparently the three of you in this building, Miss Winston, Mr. Adams, and you, were closer to Mrs. Garland than anyone else, or at least you had known each other longer."

"In a way I suppose that is true."

"I take it that you saw each other frequently and that the friendship continued to flourish after you left college."

"The apartment all three of us are living in she gave us, rent-free. She owned this house, you know."

"So—uh—your superintendent, Higgins, informed us. I suppose she came here this afternoon on a Christmas visit."

"I have no idea."

"She wasn't coming to see you?"

"I don't think so. Surely she would have called first to say that she was coming."

"Then she was coming to see Miss Winston."

"I don't know whom she was coming to see."

"That's right. Miss Winston came in just after Mrs. Garland was murdered. It's a wonder to me she didn't see the murderer; there was darned little time for him to get away. Do you think Mrs. Garland might have been intending to visit Mr. Adams?"

"I don't know. Oh, no, she wouldn't have been on the stairs in that case."

"Old friends, weren't they, Mr. Adams and Mrs. Garland?"

"Oh, of course. She had known him all her life and he was her father's most trusted friend, lived in their apartment, and he squired her all the way through college." I found myself smiling. "We all used to be jealous of the flowers he kept in her room."

"Dr. Garland didn't disapprove of this friendship?"

"Good heavens, no. Why should he?"

The detective shifted his ground. "A generous lady, Mrs. Garland, giving you all apartments rent-free."

"The most generous person I ever knew."

"Then it seems unlikely that she had any enemies in this house."

"Enemies!"

The lieutenant raised his brows. "It's customary when a person meets a violent death to imagine that it was the work of an enemy and not a friend."

"But—surely—oh, that's ridiculous! None of us could possibly—not possibly—"

"Then how do you account for the murder of your friend, Miss Lockwood?"

77

"I don't know. I supposed—you must have heard of our prowler. Miss Winston heard someone on the fourth floor and Higgins agrees that someone has been around here. The outside door is always open, you know. And Hope—Hope was apt to carry a good deal of money with her."

"You think a prowler would know that?" he asked gently.

"I have no idea. I was under the impression that muggers didn't wait to know how much their victims had. And I'm sure—that is, Miss Winston can tell you herself."

From the slight twitch of the lieutenant's lips I gathered that Winnie had given him a graphic account of the sounds she had heard and the conclusion she had drawn from them.

"And the superintendent was asking me about prowlers only—why, it was just this afternoon. He said he'd found footprints in the dust up on the fourth floor. He is going to get a new lock to put on the door after Christmas. Locking the stable, perhaps, but it might keep any stranger out."

"We've searched the fourth-floor apartment, Miss Lockwood, and the superintendent was quite right. Someone had been there, perhaps on a number of occasions, as the footprints overlap in many places." While he waited for the sergeant to catch up on his notes, Saxby lighted another cigarette. "You are sure you have seen no stranger in the halls or loitering outside the building?"

"No, I haven't."

"Quite sure?" he insisted. "Miss Winston tells us that she has frequently seen men lurking outside."

"They would be lurking," I said impatiently, and the sergeant looked up and grinned.

"The idea of a prowler who was after easy money is disproved by the fact that Mrs. Garland had over two hundred dollars in her handbag, in new bills, as though she intended the money as Christmas tips or something of the sort. She wasn't robbed. And I think we may dismiss the idea of any casual encounter with a mugger."

"Why?"

"The noose, Miss Lockwood." He went on smoothly, "Did Mrs. Garland often come here to see you?"

For the first time I hesitated. Then I admitted, "Only once before."

"Only once," the lieutenant repeated in apparent surprise, "though you were The Inseparables."

"But that was while we were in college, attending the same classes, sharing the same experiences. Now Mrs. Garland is—was married and Winnie and I both have jobs, very different kinds of jobs, so we go our own separate ways. That's only natural."

"Oh, quite," he assured me and I knew I had spoken too emphatically. "And what was the occasion for her other visit?"

"I don't know that there was anything special. She was horribly upset, of course. She had adored her father and his death was a terrible blow to her, especially as she was in precarious health herself."

"Precarious?"

"She had a fatal heart condition and only a short time left. That's why it seems so cruel, so needlessly cruel—" This time my voice shook and I had to strive for control. "And of course it wasn't just her father's death, bad as it was. But all the scandal—you knew he was Marshall Phelps?"

"Yes. Now when did you last see Mrs. Garland?"

I think I'd have been tempted to lie about that if I had not known it would be worse than useless. Winnie would have been sure to tell them that she had seen me at Hope's apartment the day before.

"Yesterday afternoon."

"Where?"

"At her apartment."

"Just a social visit?"

"She asked me to come because she had suffered a severe heart attack the night before. No one, Hope or the doctor, had expected that anything so bad could happen so soon."

There was a pause while the lieutenant's thick fingers drummed on the table. "Isn't it a fact, Miss Lockwood, that Mrs. Garland sent for you and accused you of having an affair with her husband?"

"That's not true. I wasn't. I have never even seen Larry to speak to since I left college, until I ran into him by sheer accident at a cocktail party day before yesterday. And then it was only a case of Hail and Farewell."

"Did Mrs. Garland believe that?"

"I'm sure she did—before I left her."

"Oh, then it required some convincing."

"She had been in an upset state," I explained, "and she wasn't thinking clearly. If she had, she would have known, she could not have helped knowing, that neither Larry nor I would do a thing like that to her."

"Dr. Garland was a devoted husband, was he?"

"I think the answer to that would come better from him, don't you?"

"You are undoubtedly right," he agreed cordially. "The problem is that Dr. Garland has not so far made himself available for questioning. He is not at his apartment—his wife's apartment; nor at his art gallery; he doesn't appear to have any favorite haunts. Do you have any idea of where he would likely be found?"

I shook my head, my heart beginning to pound erratically. *His wife's apartment. His wife's art gallery. He has not made himself available for questioning.* And the lieutenant had implied that Larry might be jealous of Hart's devotion to his wife. And Winnie would never have missed a God-given chance to impress on the police that Larry was an errant husband. She had probably done full justice to the gorgeous blonde.

When the telephone rang, I leaped like a gazelle. It was Roger, his voice rough with shock. "Sue, for God's sake, what has happened? There's a news bulletin on CBS that Mrs. Lawrence Garland, daughter of the late and unlamented Marshall Phelps, has been murdered in the hall of your building. Is that true?"

"Oh, Roger! Yes, it's true."

"Is she the wife of that guy you met at the party?"

"Yes."

"How did it happen?"

"I don't know yet. I don't think anyone knows. The police are here now."

"Here? You mean—with you?"

"Yes."

"Shall I come along?"

"No, no, that isn't necessary. But—thank you, Roger."

"How about a lawyer? I can get a good one up to you in the next hour, and meantime you can just sit tight, you know."

"But I don't need—" I saw the lieutenant watching me intently, making no pretense not to be following every word I said, so I did not finish.

"Sure?" Roger insisted.

"Not tonight, at any rate."

"Okay. I'll be seeing you tomorrow. And Sue—" for once he sounded almost diffident—"I wish you'd do something for me. Put on my ring—you got it, didn't you?—and say you are engaged to me. I won't hold you to it, just regard it as a kind of air-raid shelter until the bombs stop falling."

"But, Roger, that's not fair—"

"Don't say anything more. Not now. Just put it on. We don't want people getting any false ideas about you and Dr. Garland, do we?"

"No."

"You'll do as I ask?"

"I—all right, Roger."

"Good night, darling, and I'm here when you want me."

Seeing the lieutenant's raised brows, which tacitly demanded an explanation, I said, "That was Roger Mullen. He wrote the travel book for which I did the illustrations. He just heard on the news about Hope dying

81

right here in this building and he knew how I'd feel. He—I'm engaged to marry him."

For a long time the questioning went on. Part of the time the lieutenant talked about Marshall Phelps, wanting to learn what I knew about him and his tangled affairs; then his talk switched to Winnie. Was she well-to-do? No, she had to earn her living. Actually, Marshall Phelps had found her a job working for a business acquaintance of his.

"She lost it yesterday. Fired without warning. She was pretty burned up about it."

"Oh, poor Winnie! And just before Christmas too. I didn't know."

"The Inseparables?"

"I've told you that naturally we've all gone separate ways."

"Naturally."

"And Winnie and I keep different hours, so we don't meet as often as you might expect. I saw her early today but she didn't mention it."

The lieutenant stood up so abruptly that I was unprepared for his departure. "Sorry to have kept you such a long time. I know you'll be glad to rest. We'll be in touch later, of course. Don't leave town without advising us." He added without apparent irony, "Merry Christmas."

As the two men went down the stairs where Hope had lain so few hours before, I heard Lieutenant Saxby say, "I'll buy you a drink and a steak. Compliments of the season."

Winnie's television set blasted on and I went to turn on my own, wondering just what Roger had heard that had so upset him, and, in particular, why he had gathered the idea that I needed the protection of a lawyer and his ring.

I waited impatiently for the regular news and then heard a voice say briskly, "This just in. Mrs. Lawrence Garland, only child of the late Marshall Phelps, whose recent death has brought about so many stunning disclosures of widespread corruption reaching into high places, was found this afternoon, murdered, a noose imbedded in her neck, in the hallway of . . ." Static shut off the voice. I strained to hear. The words came indistinctly. I knew they said something about Winnie having discovered the body when she was on her way home from doing some belated Christmas shopping. What a fool the girl was! The police must have realized that she had no packages, that there was no trace of snow on her coat.

There was a blur of sound. Then, more distinctly, like a knell, "The dead woman's husband, Dr. Lawrence Garland, former college instructor and now manager of a Fifty-seventh Street art gallery, has so far not been located. He has not been found either in his wife's Fifth Avenue apartment or at his place of business. Friends and associates are being questioned in an endeavor to acquaint him with his wife's murder. Anyone having any information—"

Chapter 7

That night I slept fitfully, haunted by Hope's swollen and discolored face. It was nearly nine when I finally awakened fully. There was a milky light at the window and snow was still falling. This was certainly going to be a white Christmas.

I got up to bathe and dress and, because it was Christmas and Roger was coming, I put on a white wool dress, tucked a red scarf into the neck, brushed my hair into as smooth a wave as I could achieve against its determination to curl up, and slipped Roger's ring on my finger. I had never owned anything but costume jewelry, so I was no expert about real jewels, but I knew this was a valuable as well as a beautiful stone.

One thing was clear by daylight that had been confused to my tired and dazed mind the night before. Roger had guessed something about my relations with Larry when he saw us together at the cocktail party. The news story had informed him that Larry was unaccounted for and that he was under suspicion in the death of his wife. He was hell-bent on protecting me in case rumor should link our names, though why he had leaped to the conclusion that the situation was acute and that I needed the protection of his ring and of a lawyer, I could not fathom.

I switched the radio on to a news program and got the expected comments about a white Christmas and peace on earth, good will to men, followed, of course, by the latest war news from countries ostensibly at peace, and the sordid accounts of fire, theft, and slaughter in New York.

Then there came a reference to Hope's murder. At five o'clock that morning Dr. Lawrence Garland, husband of the murdered woman, had been discovered in a Turkish bath where, he admitted, he was attempting to get over a bad hangover. He was greatly shocked by the news of his wife's violent death. He had not seen her since the morning before when he had left their apartment. To his knowledge his wife had no enemies unless her death was, in some way, related to her father's affairs. They had been unusually close and Dr. Garland believed that Phelps had taken his daughter farther into his confidence than anyone else. Dr. Garland had at times been outspoken in his dislike of his father-in-law. He had no explanation to make for the murder of his wife.

I had to fight the impulse to call his apartment, to tell him I believed in him. With Hope gone, he would need assurance of someone's faith in him. But that was probably the most harmful thing I could do to him.

I put on coffee and slid some cinnamon rolls into the oven to heat. This was the first Christmas in five years that Winnie and I had not spent with Hope at the Phelps apartment. Their big tree was lighted on Christmas Eve and there was always a crackling fire on the hearth. On Christmas morning we would open the elaborately wrapped presents stacked under the tree. Christmas dinner, with chestnut-stuffed turkey and a blazing plum pudding, was served at one o'clock. Later in the afternoon Mr. Phelps presided over a punch bowl of eggnog as the drawing room gradually filled with his friends, people whose names and faces for the most part were familiar to anyone who followed the news.

On impulse I took out the package containing a white silk scarf I had got for Winnie, propped it beside the jaunty little Christmas tree Roger had sent me, and went swiftly up the stairs to tap at her door. When I had identified myself, she opened it cautiously. With her face smeared with cold cream and her hair in curlers, she was a mess.

"What is it?" she asked.

"Merry Christmas, Winnie. I wondered if you'd come down and have breakfast with me."

"Well, I—well, thanks. I'll have to get dressed first, though."

"You bet you will. I can't have you around looking like the Ghost of Christmas Past."

"Sue, why don't you ask Hart, too? He must be feeling awful."

"That's an idea. I will. See you in a few minutes."

Before going down, I went up to the fourth floor and tried the knob. The door was locked and when I put my ear to the panel, I could not hear a sound. As I came around the landing to the third floor, I saw Higgins on his way up. He gave me a quick look and I rushed into speech, which I knew, even then, was a mistake. There was no reason why I should make any explanation of my conduct.

"I just wanted to see for myself if the top-floor apartment is locked."

He nodded but made no comment and stood aside as I went down to the first floor. I realized that he was waiting to find out where I was going. He displayed an unpleasant amount of curiosity in my movements, it seemed to me.

Hart admitted me, wearing a dressing gown and bedroom slippers. He looked as though he had not slept at all, as though he had aged during the night.

"I've asked Winnie to join me for breakfast this morning. I'll bet you haven't eaten anything, either last night or this morning."

He pushed his hand through his unbrushed hair. "Coffee."

"Please join us for breakfast. Do come, Hart. It would be better than brooding all alone."

He gave me his nice smile, though he seemed to have to stretch tired muscles in order to achieve it. "That's good of you, Sue. I'd be glad to." He ran his hand over his jaw. "I'll have to shave. Five minutes."

In my own apartment I made more coffee, rescued

the cinnamon rolls, scooped out grapefruit, took eggs from the refrigerator and put slices of bacon in a pan.

When Hart came to the door, neatly dressed and freshly shaved, the place smelled appetizingly of sizzling bacon and hot bread and coffee. I directed him to set up three little tables, told him where to find the silver and napkins, and directed him to place the three dishes of grapefruit on the tables. I had just poured the eggs in the pan when Winnie arrived. She had dressed carefully but tastelessly in a red dress that added pounds to her heavy body, and on the dress glittered and flashed a horseshoe-shaped brooch set with diamonds. I stared at it unbelievingly.

"Isn't it gorgeous?" she exclaimed. "Hope gave it to me."

And that, I thought, makes you a liar, my pet. Hope would never have parted with her father's gift, her lucky piece. Never in the world.

"I remember seeing it," Hart said unexpectedly. "She was very fond of it and wore it a lot. I think she really believed it brought her luck." The look he gave Winnie indicated that I was not alone in my suspicion that she had come by it dishonestly.

Imagination raced unchecked. *If* Winnie had seen the brooch, as I had, on Hope's table; *if* she had taken advantage of a moment of inattention to steal it; *if* Hope had come here to retrieve her lucky piece, her father's gift—I came up short at the conclusion I could not help reaching.

"Pour the coffee, will you," I asked, "while I scramble the eggs?"

When I came back with a tray holding three plates of bacon and eggs and a basket of hot cinnamon rolls wrapped in a napkin, I gave Winnie her Christmas present, which she opened with little cries of "Oh, it's so pretty I can't bear to open it," and a squeal like a small child's when she opened the package and saw the scarf. Coyly she wrapped it around her neck and insisted on wearing it.

Hart crumbled a cinnamon roll and then, with an

effort, made himself taste the scrambled eggs. Apparently he realized then how much he needed food and he ate heartily. Winnie took the last of the rolls, which she buttered lavishly, with a giggling comment about watching her weight and how wicked I was to tempt her. By the time every scrap of the breakfast had disappeared, Hart's color was much better. When he had poured himself a third cup of coffee and lighted a cigarette, he sat back with a little sigh. "That was a lifesaver, Sue."

"Sue," Winnie exclaimed shrilly and I saw Hart wince with ill-concealed distaste, "Sue! That ring! Where did you get that gorgeous ring? Did Dr. Garland—"

Hart's lips tightened and I was startled by the depth of my own anger. "Roger Mullen gave me the ring, Winnie. I'm engaged to marry him."

Winnie was no sensitive plant, but she was taken aback by the sheer fury in my eyes. "Well, I'm sure—well, I certainly congratulate you, Sue. Sudden, isn't it? I mean I always thought—"

Before she could blunder farther, I said, "I've known him for nearly six months and we've been working together on his book."

"I know that's what you said."

Hart intervened. "I'm glad something good is happening to you, Sue. You deserve happiness. He's a lucky guy and I'd like to be able to tell him so. Looks and brains and guts and," his eyes drifted to Winnie, drifted away, "loyalty. That's a hard combination to beat."

I laughed. "You'll probably have a chance to tell him so. Please build me up."

Hart smiled. "I doubt if that will be needed."

"He'll be here sometime today." In spite of myself my eyes went back to that glittering brooch. There had been times in the dormitory when girls had complained that things were missing: stockings and handkerchiefs, earrings, a compact. Once Hope lost a silver bracelet she had left in a drawer but, so far as I knew, she had never been suspicious of Winnie. Or had she known and, with her usual ironic detachment, simply let it go?

I remembered Higgins's sharp command when Winnie had tried to pick up Hope's gold compact. But perhaps she was only trying to protect it. To steal from the dead! That was too ugly. But she had lied about when she came home. Her coat was dry. She had not been coming in. She must have been coming down from her own apartment. But had she found Hope dead or—or—

Abruptly I became aware that I was staring at Winnie and that both she and Hart had noticed it. "Oh, Winnie," I exclaimed, "I'm terribly sorry to hear about your job. Such a beastly shame! And just before Christmas too."

"How did you know? Did Hope tell you?"

"No, it was Lieutenant Saxby. What are you planning to do?"

Winnie shrugged plump shoulders and the diamonds flashed in multi-colored beauty on her breast. "I don't know. It's the worst possible time of year to get any kind of job, and Mr. Rogers was perfectly filthy to me. He didn't even pay me anything but one extra week. No recommendation or anything."

"I remember you told me you'd had some sort of run-in with him, but I didn't realize it was so serious."

"Because I was doing some filing and I had a letter to put in his personal file and I just happened to see this memorandum on Mr. Phelps's letterhead. I could hardly help seeing what it said and naturally I was interested, knowing him and all. And I must say you'd hardly believe a big firm like Rogers and Rogers could do such crooked business. They paid thousands of dollars to get this contract and I don't see how they'd expect to make any profit that way, or how Mr. Phelps could get it for them. Here he was always acting so important and he turns out to be just a grafter. That's all he was. And then I got fired for finding a piece of evidence that won't do his memory any good, I can tell you that."

I recalled Hope saying, "I've learned for myself that Winnie is a rat."

"You'd found other things, hadn't you?" I asked.

"Well, I kept my eyes open," Winnie admitted. "You'd be surprised at some of the stuff Mr. Phelps had in his library."

"Someone wrote to the police about Mr. Phelps's affairs and later wrote the FBI suggesting that he had been murdered. Did you do that, Winnie?"

"Well, they sat up there in that grand apartment, acting so superior to everyone, and living off the fat of the land. And no better than the Mafia, if you ask me. And Hope got Dr. Garland, and her father gave her an art gallery to keep him happy. And what do I get? A lousy job as a filing clerk for one of Phelps's business friends. Accomplices is the right word. So why shouldn't I show them up? You needn't look so disapproving and shocked, Hart. I can tell you one thing. I saw a lot that went on there."

"Such as?" he asked, his voice hard.

"For one thing the tapes that recorded everything people said when they were in the library. And I never said a word about them until last night, when I felt I owed it to myself to tell the police. As a good citizen I owed a duty to give them the real facts." She giggled. "At least some of them. A girl has a right to look after herself. The way I see it, you take your social security where you find it. You've got to remember I haven't a cent coming in."

Hart scraped back his chair. "Sorry, Sue, but I can't stand any more of this or I'll wring the girl's neck." He turned on Winnie, who pushed back on the couch, aware of the full strength of his rage. "When I think of what Hope did for you over the years—why the very apartment you are living in now you owe to her—and you could turn on her like that and try to blacken her father's name—" He made a helpless gesture and went out. I heard him running down the stairs and the slam of his door.

"Well, I must say," Winnie exclaimed, her face

flushed. "I'd never have thought Hart had it in him to be downright rude. Of course he was always practically demented about Hope and thought she was perfect. The slightest word against her was enough to set him off. I wonder how he liked living there, watching her act like the sun rose and set in that precious husband of hers. Do you realize, Sue, that Hope's murderer was right here in this building yesterday?"

"What I don't understand is how you failed to see him. By the time you—found Hope her body was still warm. You must have passed him on the stoop. Where had you been, Winnie?"

She took her time replying. "I had some last-minute shopping. When I came in I saw her there on the stairs."

"Last-minute shopping without any packages. Out in a heavy snow storm without any snow on your coat? You'll have to do better than that, Winnie. A whole lot better. You weren't coming in. You were going out."

She gave an indignant sniff. "Are you suggesting that I had anything to do with Hope's murder?"

"I don't know about that, but I do know this, Winnie. Hope never gave you that brooch. It was her favorite gift from her father and she believed it brought her luck. I saw it on the table beside her chaise longue day before yesterday, just before she quarreled with you. She was in no mood to give you a fabulously expensive and cherished gift."

"I guess you forget that she owed me something, getting me fired the way she did. But I didn't kill her. It never entered my mind to do a thing like that. I didn't want her dead. What's going to happen to us now?"

"But you lied about coming in when Hope died."

"Oh, all right, so I lied about it. But I was scared, Sue. She telephoned me and said she was coming here."

"For the brooch?"

There was a curious little silence and then Winnie said, "Yes, for the brooch. And I didn't want to see her. I was just going out, closing my door, when I heard her fall. At least I didn't know it was Hope. At least I just thought she'd stumbled over that hole in the carpet. So I was going to go back in the apartment and then I thought I'd rather see her on the stairs. She couldn't make a scene where people could hear her. So I went down. And—there she was."

"But who—?"

"There was no one in the hall, Sue."

"But someone had to be there! You must have seen or heard someone or something."

Her eyes narrowed and the color drained out of her face. "Let me alone! It's no business of yours!" She got up from the couch, walked haughtily toward the door, came back to retrieve her Christmas gift and even the wrappings, rolling up the satin ribbon carefully. "I can use this again," she said absently and stalked out of the room.

Peace on earth, good will to men.

I cleared away the breakfast dishes and opened the window briefly to let out the smoke from Hart's cigarettes—I had never before known him to be a chain smoker. Then, because I could not help it, I unlocked the desk drawer and took out Larry's sketch of me, with my hair, which he said he wanted to touch, curled up tight, and that betraying glow in my eyes.

There was a tap at the door. Roger at last! Hastily I returned the picture to the drawer, locked it, and slid the key under the clock on the mantel.

But it was not Roger. It was Maxwell Higgins, once more neatly dressed in a business suit. "May I come in for a moment?"

"Yes, of course. Is anything wrong?"

He stood surveying me with a detached sort of interest and I remembered how he had watched me test the door and put my ear to the panel.

"I've been trying to figure out what I ought to do," he said. "This is a calculated risk." He opened his wallet and I read the card.

"Federal Bureau of Investigation?"

He nodded.

"I think you'd better sit down." When he had complied, I said, "Would you like some coffee?" and when he looked pleased, I went out to put on a fresh pot. I called from the kitchen, "But what on earth has Hope's murder to do with the FBI? Oh, of course, you were here in the house before she was killed. I don't understand."

"The FBI is looking into the affairs of Marshall Phelps, particularly as they might have been concerned with the suicide of Graham Woods. Miss Lockwood, that was the boldest and the most successful attempt ever made to eliminate a presidential candidate, with the exception of the assassination of Robert Kennedy."

"But why look for evidence in this house?"

"The only tangible assets Phelps left were his Fifth Avenue apartment, the art gallery, and this house. Actually, the two latter, as you probably know, he gave to his daughter. We can understand the art gallery, but this house? What was it for? That's what we want to know."

"Oh, I can answer that! I was there when Mr. Phelps gave it to Hope last Christmas. She was surprised at him giving her an old run-down building, but he told her that most of this block was to be razed to make way for a big apartment building and this house was the only holdout. He wanted her to keep it until the builders were forced to give her her own price. He told her—something—I can't remember the exact words—but that she'd be surprised to see how valuable this building was. I remember he laughed as though it were a joke."

A light flashed in his rather pale eyes. "Oh! And he didn't explain further?"

"He just spoke about the increase in value if Hope held onto it."

"And then you all moved in."

"Well, it wasn't quite like that. Hope wanted to give me this apartment—" I broke off. I couldn't explain that she was trying in her own way to make up to me for losing Larry. "She knew I had no money and no very lucrative job and she knew it would be a great help to live without having to pay rent."

"And Miss Winston?"

At that moment I wasn't feeling very charitable toward Winnie. "When she found out that Hope had given me an apartment, she put in a claim to have one too. At least I suppose that is what happened."

"I see. And Mr. Adams?"

"That was different. He'd been Mr. Phelps's closest associate, it was the only job he'd ever held, and now he's out of work and, because of all the scandals, he can't use Mr. Phelps's name as a recommendation in looking for anything else. Hope thought it was the least she could do for him, as he had been victimized through no fault of his own."

"Why couldn't he continue to live, as I understand he did for many years, in the Phelps apartment?"

"When Hope came here to see me, she said she would probably have to sell the apartment. There seems to be no money left to keep it going. Mr. Higgins, I can't understand. They lived so lavishly. What on earth happened to all the money?"

"That's a problem that troubles a lot of people, particularly the Treasury boys. The stuff may be hoarded; it may be in a numbered account in a Swiss bank. It's about the only problem that isn't my headache. Mrs. Garland came to see you just before Mr. Adams moved in, didn't she? I remember seeing her when she arrived. A pretty woman in mourning." He repeated, "Pretty," and I remembered how we had last seen her. "I wish you'd tell me everything you remember about that meeting, Miss Lockwood."

I thought back. "I was on my way to deliver some illustrations and as I opened the outside door, Hope was just coming in."

"Did she say that she was coming to see you?"

"Well, who else? Winnie was at work and Hart hadn't moved in yet. That was the day Hope suggested turning the first-floor apartment over to him. There wasn't anyone else for her to see."

Higgins pinched his lower lip between thumb and forefinger. When he spoke, he took me aback. "Was she carrying a large handbag like the one she had yesterday?"

"Yes, she always did."

"Empty, except for a clip of bills, keys, compact and handkerchief?"

"I don't know. I don't remember her opening the bag while she was with me and I don't understand what you are getting at."

"I'm groping. One thing seems to be fairly clear, Miss Lockwood. Mrs. Garland was intensely interested in this house. It had a special meaning for her. I've searched every square inch of the place; heaven help me, even going so far as to tap the walls looking for hidden cupboards, and I can't find a thing."

"Oh, you must be Winnie's prowler!"

He grinned and seemed much more likable and approachable. "No, I am not Winnie's prowler, but someone has been up on the fourth floor." He added, "Just as you were this morning."

"Honestly, I just tried the lock. I'm braver by daylight than I am in the dark and, after yesterday, and Hope—I wanted to be sure no one was getting in there."

"I don't think anyone has been hiding there. But there is something—you're sure that Mr. Phelps said nothing except that his daughter would be surprised by the value of the house?"

"So far as I can see, Mr. Higgins, you suspect Hope of being the one who has been getting into that fourth-floor apartment. But why on earth would she? The place is empty, I assume. And why would anyone kill her for coming to her own house?"

"There are three people living in this house; probably, aside from her father and her husband, the three closest to her."

"But you don't believe that I—that one of us—"

"I could," and he was not smiling, "make out a good case against every one of you."

I went out to unplug the coffeepot and brought back

a tray with cups and saucers, sugar and cream. I set it on the table in front of the couch where Higgins was sitting, and when I had handed him his cup, I set my own on the desk beside my chair.

"I don't know whether you are supposed to drink coffee with a murderer," I said disagreeably.

"There's no rule about it." He grinned at me. He sipped coffee cautiously and set it down to cool. "Let's start with Miss Winston. That woman interests me greatly."

"She would be flattered if she knew that."

"For years she has been the recipient of exceptional kindness from Mrs. Garland. She was one of The Inseparables at college. Phelps provided her with a job when she graduated, his daughter gave her an apartment rent-free. But Miss Winston, as we have learned from college people who remember her, has an unengaging habit of pilfering small objects not only from her friends but from stores. Oh, yes," he went on, seeing my surprise, "Mr. Phelps several times extricated her from what might have been very awkward situations."

College people who remember her. So we were all being investigated and had been ever since the murder.

"This morning I wondered—"

"The brooch," he prompted me.

"How do you know?" After a pause I exclaimed, "This apartment has been bugged! Of all the outrageous, inexcusable invasions of privacy!"

"We are looking for something more important than your privacy, Miss Lockwood."

"In the long run there is nothing more important for an American citizen than to hang onto his privacy."

"That's an ethical question I can't answer. I use the tools I am given."

"So you heard me accuse Winnie of stealing that brooch."

"Yes."

"How long has the apartment been bugged?"

"Sometime. A week."

"Then I suppose you also heard—" I remembered the evening when only a wrong number had prevented Roger from making love to me. I felt my cheeks scorch.

Higgins did not pretend to misunderstand. "Sometimes telephones have their uses, Miss Lockwood."

He was outrageous, of course, but unexpectedly I found myself laughing, free of embarrassment.

"And I gather that you are planning to marry Mr. Mullen." Higgins looked at the opal glowing on my finger. He switched smoothly. "Now to go on with my case against Miss Winston. She had a bitter quarrel with Mrs. Garland shortly after you left the Phelps apartment day before yesterday. Her maid overheard it. Mrs. Garland accused her friend of giving the police and the FBI anonymous information she had gathered from prying into the files on her job as well as material she had filched from the apartment itself. Apparently it was Mrs. Garland who was responsible for her friend being fired. She was also going to have her dispossessed from her apartment here. It seems to me that Miss Winston may well have been in a mood to revenge herself on her erstwhile friend.

"We have her own confession to you that she stole the brooch. If we assume that Mrs. Garland came here to retrieve it—and Miss Winston was obviously afraid to face that meeting, she was doing her best to get out of the house before Mrs. Garland came—we have an explosive situation."

"But, Mr. Higgins, Hope was strangled with a noose. Granted that Winnie knew she was going to be confronted, she could never have prepared a noose and killed Hope like that. Her one thought was to get out of the house."

Higgins shrugged. "The crowning mystery is that, according to her story, she found Mrs. Garland within a few brief seconds—a minute or two at most—after her murder, and yet she saw and heard nothing."

When I had no comment to make Higgins said, "And so we come to the case against Adams. If Mrs. Garland informed Miss Winston that she was coming here, we may assume she also informed Mr. Adams."

"Hart!" I expelled a long breath in sheer exasperation. "I wish I could make you understand. He's the last person, the very last person, ever to injure Mrs. Garland. He's been just plain besotted about her for years and years. He wanted to marry her and her father hoped they would marry. He wouldn't have harmed her in any conceivable way. Why he fainted when he realized that she was dead. And he had no reason for killing her."

"I wonder," Higgins said thoughtfully, "if you can look at this thing with any detachment. You've known these people so long that, like a familiar painting on the wall, you no longer see them as they are—if you ever did. Mr. Adams, according to our information, was asked by Mrs. Garland to act as her husband's best man. Has it ever occurred to you that was a singularly cruel thing to demand of him? He had to live in an apartment with a honeymoon couple, day and night. If you are right about his feeling for Mrs. Garland, that must have been sheer hell. All of a sudden he was asked to leave."

"And that provides a motive for murder?"

"Would you say Adams is a stupid man, Miss Lockwood?"

"Not at all. Not brilliant, perhaps, but an excellent brain. Painstaking rather than creative. I suppose his chief weakness was his complete, blind hero worship where Marshall Phelps was concerned."

"Can you make yourself believe that an intelligent man could work closely with Phelps for years and not even suspect he was carrying on shady dealings?"

"I've thought about that a lot, Mr. Higgins, since Mr. Phelps died and all the discoveries have been made, and it seems to me that Hart was the best possible cover Mr. Phelps could have had. He is so transparently honest that no one could possibly suspect Phelps while Hart was there, serving as a kind of front man for him."

"That's a good point. Still if we are to assume that Winnie Winston, who is not intelligent, could pick up damning information at the Phelps apartment by some aimless prowling around, I find it difficult to believe that Adams failed to do so."

"Well, I refuse to suspect Hart and that's all there is to it."

"And then," Higgins went on, drinking his coffee with more confidence, "there is the case against you."

"Of course," I said cordially. "And what is my motive for killing my best friend?"

"Dr. Garland," Higgins told me. "Mrs. Garland's maid heard her accuse you of having an affair with her husband. The television station let me have a glimpse of that film they taped of the cocktail party at which you 'accidentally' met Dr. Garland. That was quite an explosive moment, wasn't it? Generated enough electricity to handle the energy crisis."

I moved my hand restlessly and the opal glowed under the light.

"Oh, yes," Higgins said softly, "you are engaged to marry Mr. Mullen, aren't you? My congratulations, Miss Lockwood." He got up and then sat down again. "Is there anything, any single thing about this house you haven't told me?"

I shook my head. "All I know I've told you over and over, that Mr. Phelps said it was not to be sold until it had increased in value."

"Nothing else? No matter how trivial?"

"Nothing. Oh, the fireplaces, of course."

"What about the fireplaces?" he asked alertly, the cat at the mousehole sensing movement.

"Just some defect in the flues so that it would be dangerous to have fires. But, of course, we haven't needed them, especially since you came and kept the building so much warmer."

"I see. Thank you very much. I'd appreciate it if you didn't find it necessary to refer to my real position here. And thank you for the coffee."

I listened to him as he went up the stairs to Winnie's

apartment and heard her agitated question. Poor Winnie! She was in for a tough time. I wondered vaguely if it was true that she was some sort of kleptomaniac.

Only one thought obsessed me, however. It was all very well for Maxwell Higgins to outline the flimsy cases against Winnie and Hart and me. What he had not done was to outline the case against Larry, and that was the most ominous fact of all.

Chapter 8

When he arrived with Sergeant Clark shortly after Higgins had gone to see Winnie, Lieutenant Saxby's manner was unlike what it had been before. He rejected almost rudely my offer of coffee and while I hung his heavy coat and that of the sergeant over the bathroom rod to dry, I tried to summon up as casual a manner as possible because his attitude had changed so drastically.

"It's too bad you have to work on Christmas Day," I said when I had returned to the living room.

Saxby shrugged heavy shoulders. "I'm divorced and I have no family, so it doesn't matter much to me. Anyhow, I'll get New Year's Eve, and that's always tough on a cop. Too many people drinking in the New Year and one thing and another." He leaned forward in his chair and his expression was not pleasant at all. "Miss Lockwood, why did you deliberately lie to me about Mrs. Garland's condition?"

I was so surprised I could only gape at him.

"That heart condition. What a very moving story you told me about being summoned to your friend's side after she had suffered a severe heart attack. Now I'd like the truth for a change."

"But I didn't lie about it! Hope herself told me—oh, months ago, in the spring before we left college—that she had only a short time to live, that her heart had suffered permanent damage from rheumatic fever. And when I saw her the other day, she had just had a severe heart attack. Her own physician, Dr. Partridge, could testify to that."

101

"We've seen the autopsy report. Would it surprise you to know that Mrs. Garland had a perfectly sound heart? We've talked to Dr. Partridge who says she had a misleading look of fragility, but she was the wiry type who usually outlives her generation by years, and that she had more physical stamina than half the people in her age group whom he knew."

The whole truth seemed to rush on me in a moment. Hope had deliberately lied to me, she had made that desperate appeal to my sympathy in order to persuade me to give up Larry.

"So why did you really go to see Mrs. Garland the other afternoon?" Saxby put up a hand warningly. "It was not because she had had a heart attack. Let's see if you can't do better this time."

"She told me she'd had an attack and I believed her."

"Speak up, Miss Lockwood. The sergeant can't hear you."

"I believed her," I said more loudly. "I never dreamed—it never occurred to me that she was not telling me the truth."

"And why would she have told you this touching story?"

I could not answer. I could not say, "She wanted me to give up the man I loved so she could marry him." If they were already suspicious of Larry, this would provide him with a powerful motive. That is, if he too had discovered the trick she had played on us.

"Well, Miss Lockwood?"

I shook my head.

"Speak up, please. The sergeant can't take down gestures."

"I don't know."

"Perhaps I can help you. You see we know what happened when Mrs. Garland sent for you. She accused you of having an affair with her husband." Again Saxby put up his big hand. "Yes, we've gone over this before and you have stated that it was not true. But we've learned from other sources that up to a few weeks before Garland married Miss Phelps he was almost constantly with you."

Other sources. That would be Winnie, of course.

"Suppose, Miss Lockwood, that this young lady whom you called your best friend and the most generous person you ever knew, wanted to marry Garland and figured out a good way to get you out of the picture—and you'd provide tough competition for most women—and she spun you this yarn to make you bow out."

I made no comment and after waiting for me to speak he went on. "Now suppose that Garland finds out in some way what his wife has been up to. He doesn't, by all accounts, like his father-in-law; he probably doesn't like having to live in his apartment; he's got a nice art gallery to run as he pleases if he can just get rid of his wife and you are still—available."

"This all sounds pretty silly to me, Lieutenant," I said as steadily as I could.

"Would you regard Mrs. Garland as a quarrelsome woman?"

"Not at all. She had an aloofness, a kind of detachment. She never quarreled."

He raised his brows and made a grimace of incredulity. "Now that sounds odd to me. The day before she was murdered she had a bang-up quarrel with you, accusing you of trying to take her husband; she had another quarrel not long afterwards with Miss Winston, accusing her of spying into her father's affairs and threatening to have her thrown out of her apartment. And to top her detached, aloof sort of day she had a regular slugging match with her husband. Accused him of making a fool of himself and of her by the way he had looked at you at some party, accused him of carrying on with a blonde, accused him of letting his obsessive hatred of her father carry him too far. She threatened to sell the art gallery and leave him high and dry if he didn't toe the mark. Aloof is not the word I'd use for the way she carried on the day before someone murdered her."

I waited, hiding my hands behind me because I could not control their shaking.

"Now, according to the servants, Garland slammed out of her room and no one saw him until he left the apartment next morning. According to his testimony, he did not see his wife again after that quarrel, which, by the way, he does not deny. He says he went to the gallery for a few hours and, as there was no business, he closed up shop and started on a little plain and fancy pub-crawling and ended, some hours later, in a Turkish bath."

"Well, that's probably what happened," I said, realizing that he was waiting for me to make some comment.

"According to one theory," Saxby said, his eyes hard on mine, "Garland came to this house where his wife found him—or followed him—and he put her permanently out of the way."

"I don't believe it."

Again he made that odd grimace, twisting his mouth in a kind of wry amusement. "We'll soon know," he said easily. "We are interested in Dr. Garland's movements and we've just begun to question him. We know how to question. Sooner or later he will break. Believe me, Miss Lockwood, he will break." He grinned. "And when the D.A. gets a good look at you he won't have to go far for a motive."

"It's a flimsy motive," I assured him, with growing confidence. "And Dr. Garland may be a talented man, but he doesn't add invisibility to the list of his accomplishments. If he came to this house, Higgins would have seen him. He sees everyone who passes his window."

"Not unless he stands there twenty-four hours a day. It's one thing to be on the lookout; it's another to provide uninterrupted surveillance. But in a way that is a shame," Saxby said almost jovially. "I don't like to see women involved in murder. But if Dr. Garland didn't kill his wife on your account, it seems most likely that he had an accomplice to do it for him, Miss Lockwood."

104

"I then raced up to my room without Winnie seeing me. Of all the silly fishing expeditions!" I think he was taken aback by my new-found confidence. "None of this makes sense, and I think you know it. I was not having an affair with Lawrence Garland. I never at any time had an affair with him. If you are trying to establish me as the motive for Hope's murder, you are looking in the wrong place. I am engaged to marry Roger Mullen and we plan to travel and collaborate on some books, which he will write and I will illustrate. We've already done one together. This is the truth as far as any possible relationship with Larry Garland is concerned. You can ask our publisher, who will tell you about the plans being made for the trip to the Scandinavian countries in the spring."

Saxby locked eyes with me as a wrestler might try to wrap his arms around his antagonist, but I did not waver and returned the look steadily. Every word I had said could be proved and I had the confidence that came from knowing it.

"Okay, I'm inclined to believe you. I'd like to believe you. You could easily be trouble for a man," and he grinned, "but I hope it's not that kind. I think you're straight. At least I hope to God you are. But if—" he looked around for an ashtray and I went to get one for him— "if," he went on, after thanking me and crushing out his cigarette, "Garland didn't kill his wife, with or without your assistance, what was it all about? If she wasn't killed because her husband wanted to get rid of her, she must have been killed because she was involved in her father's affairs, which opens a wide field, a hell of a wide field. There was even a hint that her old man was murdered too, and Garland, from what we hear on all sides, hated his father-in-law and made no secret of the fact."

There was a tap on the door and I went to open it. Roger stood smiling at me, holding a small transparent box containing two milky gardenias. He looked for the opal ring and then took me in his arms and kissed me. "Merry Christmas, darling," he said, and then saw the two policemen and, in spite of the plain clothes, he recognized their function at once.

He came in and let me take his snowy overcoat. I introduced the three men and went to hang his coat with the others. I could hear Saxby say something and as I came back, I heard Roger reply, "Thank you very much. I know I'm a lucky man." He sat down calmly, making himself at home and also making clear that he intended to stay while I was being questioned. His manner could not have been more casual, but there was a hard line around his mouth I had not seen before and a tension which was unusual in the easy-going man.

"I suppose you are looking into Mrs. Garland's death," he said. "I gathered from the news reports that she is another victim of a mugger. It's a blow to Miss Lockwood, you know, as they have been close friends for years."

"So I understand. We have, of course, considered the possibility of a mugger, but certain factors seem to make that unlikely." Saxby went on calmly as though it were quite in order for him to be revealing these matters, and I saw Sergeant Clark's surprise. "For one thing, Mrs. Garland was not robbed. She had over two hundred dollars in her handbag as well as a gold compact, which seems to be valuable. Another thing is the noose. Not a mugger's weapon. Savors of premeditation, wouldn't you think? And still another thing—" Saxby looked at Roger. "You see, Mr. Mullen, according to one highly reliable witness, no one was observed coming in."

I could see the shock take hold. Then Roger said, "I assume you are quite sure of your facts."

"We aren't positive, but it seems a strong possibility. This particular witness has had the house under close observation for some time."

"Why?"

Saxby hadn't expected the question. "The police had reason to be interested in the place," he answered vaguely.

I put in recklessly, "The FBI thinks that Marshall

Phelps was using this house for some purpose, perhaps he had hidden something here. And there's a strong chance that Hope knew about it. Her father had a habit of confiding in her."

I had not realized how tense Roger was until I saw him relax. "Then it would appear that Mrs. Garland's death was related to her father's affairs rather than to any personal considerations."

"That's one theory." I could see that Saxby was doing a slow burn because Higgins had revealed his identity to me.

"In that case," Roger said smoothly, "I can't see why you must question Miss Lockwood. She had no knowledge of Mr. Phelps's affairs."

"Did Phelps ever discuss any business matters with you?" Saxby asked.

I smiled at the absurdity of the idea. "Our relations were completely and solely social. It was hard to believe, even when I stayed at the apartment for fairly long periods of time, that he conducted his business there. Of course, the library where he worked had a separate outside entrance, so we never saw his business acquaintances come and go."

"As I recall the news stories," Roger put in, "that door was found unlocked the morning after Phelps's death, and someone had ransacked the place. Looks to me like the work of an outsider."

"It certainly appeared to be," Saxby agreed. "The police too have been aware of that possibility or that red herring, Mr. Mullen."

"Sorry. I'm sure you know your own business without any helpful suggestions from the sidelines."

Saxby turned to me. "Did you ever hear Phelps speak about any tapes he had in the library?"

"Tapes? No. Oh, when Winnie and Hart Adams were here for breakfast she said she had known about them. I think she was taunting Hart because she knew more about them than he did."

"Winnie. Is that the lady who prowls around?"

"Well—apparently."

Saxby got up to leave and the sergeant scrambled to his feet, shoving the notebook into his pocket. At a nod from me Roger went to get their coats.

"You know," Saxby remarked, "I think your friend Miss Winston had better look out for herself. She could be letting herself in for a lot of trouble."

"You'd better tell her yourself. She'd take it more seriously from you than from me."

"I intend to." Unexpectedly Saxby smiled at me before going up the stairs to Winnie's apartment. "I'll be seeing you."

"And now I think," and Roger sounded like a stranger, "you'd better tell me what this is all about. Just what happened to your friend and what do the police want with you?" He wasn't at all his usual easy-going, lighthearted self. I had never before known him to be so serious.

So I told him the whole thing, as fully and accurately as I could. When I had finished, he began to prowl up and down the room. Something in his restless movements reminded me of Hope the day she had come there. Why had she come? We had met by chance at the door, but she may not have intended to see me at all. And that was the day she had implied that Larry might have had a hand in her father's death.

After standing at the window with his back to me for some time Roger came to put his hands on my shoulders. He did not attempt to kiss me. He simply made me look at him. "Just how important is Garland to you?" His eyes held mine, demanding an answer, and I owed him that. His ring had protected me from the police, persuading them that I was not involved emotionally with Larry.

"I don't know," I admitted. "That's the hell of it, Roger. I don't know."

"All right," he said at last, "let's have it."

So I told him about having Larry as a lecturer in art, about our accidental meeting in the rain, and how we had begun to see each other frequently. Then Hope had come to tell me that she had a fatal heart condition and only a short time to live, and she wanted Larry. She said it would almost make up for having so little time for happiness. As a result I had broken with Larry, writing to him because I didn't dare see him or all my defenses would have broken down. I had never seen him again, except on three occasions: once at his wedding, a second time when we were waiting for a traffic light to change but we were on opposite sides of the street, and the third was the accidental encounter at the cocktail party.

"Go on," Roger said.

"I didn't know, until the lieutenant told me just now, that Hope never had a bad heart condition. She was in perfectly sound health, according not only to her regular physician but to the autopsy findings."

"I see. Go on."

I told him that Higgins, whom I had taken for a superintendent, was an FBI agent, looking into Marshall Phelps's affairs, in the belief that some evidence was to be found in the brownstone. I told him of Winnie's revelations of what she had learned on her job and in her prowling around the Phelps library and her prying into office files. And I told him that Larry was being questioned at this very minute because the police suspected him of having a hand in his wife's murder, with or without my assistance.

"But he didn't do it," I said. "He didn't do it!"

"You're going to hate me for this, Sue. So far as I can make out, you see this guy Garland as a kind of Cary Grant who sweeps all women off their feet. Okay, maybe he is. Now you've given me a picture of you sacrificing yourself for your friend Hope, who was obviously double-crossing you. Given her kind of father and training, it was probably the only way she knew to operate."

Someone else had said something like that. Oh, of course, the classmate who had said that Hope arranged for the art gallery in order to get rid of student competition, and, she had said, "Like father, like daughter."

"But let's take a detached look at this guy Garland,

not through your rosy spectacles but from a man's standpoint. He turns from you to Hope Phelps within a matter of a few weeks, though he had never noticed her before. He claims to hate her father's guts but he settles down tamely in his apartment and at his expense. He claims to love teaching and says he would never want another job but he resigns from the faculty and runs a commercial art gallery owned by his wife. For my money, my darling, your precious Garland is the lowest kind of heel. He may or may not be a murderer but he acts as much like a kept man as anyone I've come across in a long time, and if he has a will of his own, there is no scrap of evidence to show it. He drifts, doing what comes easiest."

"Is that the way you really see him?"

"It's the way any self-respecting man would see him. And there's another thing. You won't believe it now but you are lucky to be out of this mess. Any guy who would turn you down for the sake of that baby-face whose picture I saw in the paper, without putting up a hell of a fight to keep you—"

"He didn't turn me down," I said, my pride stung. "I was the one who broke with him."

"And he just took it? No, Sue, he's not the man for you."

"And I suppose you are?" I said rather childishly.

He took me in his arms then, but again he did not kiss me. Roger was always sensitive and quick to understand my moods. He pressed his cheek hard against mine.

And only then did I remember that the room was bugged and that every word we had said had been recorded.

Chapter 9

The day after Christmas is, in a sense, like the morning after death in that poem of Emily Dickinson's. It's a time of letdown, of picking up the wastepaper and putting away the presents, a time of settling the bills and facing the New Year.

An early call from the store sent me out in the heavy snowstorm. They had run big ads in the Sunday papers about a holiday sale; a crowd of women, undeterred by the weather, had come to look at the glamorous evening dresses, drastically reduced in price, and which the department head had thought would go with a better swing if they were modeled. So far as I know, the idea of modeling sales clothes had never been tried, but it proved to be a smashing success.

For hours I walked and turned and answered questions about material and colors. There was barely time to change from one outfit to another and I was on my feet most of the day, stopping only once to kick off my shoes with a groan of relief and drink some black coffee while a smaller girl modeled clothes for teenagers.

For the most part there was no time to think of the brownstone house and what had happened there. The prominence of Hope Phelps Garland's name had dwarfed the others and I had appeared in the news only as living in the house where the murder had taken place. Only the department head seemed to recognize the address as mine, and she made a passing reference to what must have been an unpleasant experience, not knowing that I had been acquainted with Hope. What did arouse curiosity in the employees was the opal ring. That made a sensation.

"I suppose," the department head remarked in resignation, "this means you'll be leaving us soon. I ought to have known that you'd be too good to last. Do you realize that you've sold at least four of every model you've had on today? And how some of the purchasers are going to look in them! However, I gather they manage to see themselves as they'd like to look."

On the whole, though my very bones felt tired when I got home that evening, after having had practically no sleep for two nights, I was grateful for the respite from my gnawing anxiety, though I found it waiting for me when I had changed to a robe and soft slippers and stretched out on the couch. That night I did not try to find a record that would suit my mood. When the ring came, I got up with a groan and padded over to silence the telephone.

"I've been trying to get you all day," Roger said, his voice hoarse with strain. "If you hadn't answered this time, I was going over to the precinct to find out what the hell had happened to you."

"Oh, I'm sorry you've been worried, Roger! I got a call from the store and I've been modeling all day. I've practically worn my feet down to the ankles."

"I'll be along in a few minutes to take you out to dinner."

"Oh, no!" I exclaimed, appalled. "Not tonight. I can't move one more step. I'm going to scramble an egg, take a leisurely bath, and go to bed, and I plan to sleep for twelve hours."

"Well, I—are you sure, Sue? I wouldn't keep you out late. I know you're tired."

"I can't. The very thought of getting dressed again is more than I can face."

"All right, darling. Will you be working tomorrow?"

"No, thank God. Oh, but there's one nice thing. I was told today that by the end of the year—that's this week—I'm going to get a lovely bonus, a commission on the dresses I've helped to sell."

He laughed. "In that case, you ought to take me out to dinner. I'll call you in the morning."

"Not too early."

He laughed again. "Not too early. This laughter isn't a sign of rejoicing because I can't see you tonight, it's sheer relief that you are all safe and sound. I'll pick you up for lunch tomorrow. We'll go to one of those restaurants where we can see the skating and the big Christmas tree at Rockefeller Center."

I carried out my program, ate lightly, took a long and leisurely bath, using my favorite scented bath oil, and came back, wrapped in a warm robe, to lie on the couch and listen to a Haydn quartet. For twenty minutes or so I felt at peace, my mind as well as my body at rest, and then I went to bed, determined to sleep. My eyelids felt tight and my throat muscles were tense.

For a long time I stared into the dark and neither my preparations for the night nor the weariness of the day's work were of any avail to make me sleep. At last I got up and hunted through the medicine cabinet for sleeping pills, took two, and went back to bed. Insensibly I drifted into sleep—deep sleep.

Into my dreams there came the sound of sleigh bells that tinkled on and on, and once a heavy thump from Winnie's apartment, indicating that she had dropped something. I realized then that the sleigh bells had been the tinkling of my chandelier as Winnie walked around in her heavy-footed manner, making as much noise as though she were moving furniture. I dropped back to sleep.

II

Next morning saw the beginning of the nightmare. It was after ten when I awakened fully. Several times I had half roused and then drifted pleasantly back to sleep. I was still groggy from the unaccustomed sleeping pills, but after a shower and a cup of coffee I felt better for the long and heavy sleep. My legs and feet no longer ached and I was aware of a sense of well-being. All the forebodings of the night before seemed to have dissipated.

After a breakfast of grapefruit, blueberry muffins, and more coffee I felt ready for anything. Anyhow, I was aware that I could not afford to be at low ebb, mentally or physically. I might be in need of everything I had.

How great that need was to be, I learned before long. I had dressed carefully in the red suit, which was becoming, and which added a defiant touch of gaiety to my appearance, and I had just touched my wrists and throat with my favorite perfume when I heard the tap at the door.

Eleven o'clock. Roger must really be worried about me to come so early. But it was Higgins, Higgins again in jeans and red flannel shirt, a crease between his brows.

"Miss Lockwood," he said so urgently that I looked at him in surprise, "I'm sorry to disturb you, but I'd be grateful if you'd come up with me to Miss Winston's apartment."

"Why? Is anything wrong?"

"Well, I can't very well break in and scare the life out of her. She's a very nervous lady."

"But why should you break in?"

"She didn't put out her trash last night. I've knocked several times and called but she doesn't answer. I thought if you came along to reassure her—"

"She's probably tired out. She must have been moving furniture half the night."

"She was? If you'll come, please."

Alarmed by his manner rather than by any fear for Winnie, I followed him up the stairs. He knocked at the door several times with increasing loudness, almost banging, and I began to share his feeling that something was wrong. Then he shouted. "Miss Winston! It's Higgins. Are you all right?"

He turned to me and I called, "Winnie! Winnie, it's Sue. Please open the door. We're worried about you."

The silence dragged on. At last Higgins said, "We'll have to break in."

"But she not only has a key, she has a bolt and a chain. I don't see how anyone could get in."

"If we can't open this, I'll try the fire escape at the back and smash a window if necessary." Tentatively he turned the knob and the door swung open. For a moment, Higgins having thrust himself in front of me, we stood staring at the room. It had been ransacked. Even the couch cushions had been slashed. Someone had searched every inch of the place and done it ruthlessly, with no regard to damage.

Pushing me out of range, Higgins said, "Stay here, please," and opened the bedroom door. From the way he stood unmoving, his face set, I knew what must have happened before he stepped forward out of sight. In a minute he came back and went to the telephone. "I want a policeman. This is a homicide."

I moistened my lips. "She's dead?"

"Very," he said succinctly.

"You're quite sure? There isn't anything we can do?"

"I'm sure. You had better go down to your own apartment, Miss Lockwood, and wait there." As I started out, secretly relieved that I need not view Winnie's body, he added, "Don't leave the building, please." It wasn't the superintendent speaking now, it was the FBI agent.

"How—was she killed?"

"She was strangled."

"A noose—like Hope?"

"No, a white silk scarf."

My Christmas present! Rationally there was no reason why that should make it worse, but it did. I turned blindly and made my way downstairs and almost at once the whole thing began again: the arrival of a patrol car, the tramping of feet up and down the stairs, the roar of motors and the sound of sirens as men from the homicide squad arrived: photographer, doctor, fingerprint men, the whole paraphernalia, followed by an alert-looking young man who, I learned later, was from the district attorney's office.

I couldn't sit in that apartment, knowing that Winnie lay upstairs where my white scarf had choked out her life! Her face, like Hope's, would be swollen and discolored. I couldn't sit there another moment.

I went out to find several policemen on the stairs and the door of Winnie's apartment stood wide open. One of the men demanded sharply who I was and where I was going, though, seeing I had no handbag and no topcoat, he must have realized I was not attempting to leave the building. I explained that I was on my way down to see Hart Adams, who was a friend of mine as well as of Winifred Winston, the girl who had just been killed. I didn't want to be alone any longer.

After some hesitation the policeman nodded and warned me not to leave the building without permission.

I knocked at Hart's door and then knocked a second time. What with the voices, the tramping feet, the sirens and the cars double-parked outside, I did not see how he could avoid knowing that something was going on.

I banged on the door and shouted, "Hart! Hart! It's Sue." And then, like Higgins at Winnie's door, I asked, strain in my voice, "Are you all right?"

That brought a couple of policemen to my side. "Anything wrong, lady?"

"I don't know. He should be here, but he doesn't answer. And after what happened to Winnie—"

"Maybe he's gone out. He's probably at work this time of day."

"He's not working. He's out of a job. And in this weather he wouldn't go out unless he had to."

The two men exchanged glances and then one of them said, "We'll see if we can get in." He turned the knob and, as in Winnie's apartment, the door swung open at his touch. And, as in Winnie's apartment, the living room was a shambles. Hart lay sprawled on the floor.

I clung to the door, swaying, saying, "Oh, no! Oh, no!" in a kind of senseless babble.

"Okay, lady," one of the men said, "you'd better get up to your own apartment. We'll handle this."

The other one exclaimed, "He's dead!—No, by God, he's still alive, but he's unconscious and his head is a bloody mess. Get the Doc down here at the double, will you, Sim?"

The man called Sim took my arm and helped me up to my own door. "You just sit there and take it easy." Then I heard him call, "Is Doc still there? . . . Okay, we've got another customer. The guy is alive but that is about all."

I collapsed on a chair near the door and sat staring at the floor, not even thinking. Hope! Winnie! Hart! I found myself repeating the three names over and over, a meaningless incantation, as once, in a moment of unbearable crisis, I found myself going over and over a silly, popular tune.

At a tap on the door I called "Come in," and a young man wearing a trench coat, a sharp-faced chap with bright eyes, came in and closed the door. "You Miss Lockwood?"

"Yes."

"You a friend of the woman who was murdered upstairs?"

"Yes."

"What happened, do you know?"

I sat up, trying to shake off shock, to pull my shattered wits together, realizing that this questioning was not like the kind from Lieutenant Saxby.

"Who are you?"

"*Daily Record*. I've been keeping an eye on this house, thinking it might pay off, as long as Higgins seems to have it staked out. Things happen here, don't they? What about the guy on the first floor? This place seems to be like a pest-house."

"Mr.—whoever you are—I have no comment to make. Please go now."

"Aw, lady, don't be like that! Taking the food right

out of my mouth. Sending me out into the storm. Just give me a story. I'll get your picture in the paper. You'd photograph real nice too. Beautiful women are at a premium these days; that's why the gals have to strip to attract any attention. And I'll bet you do that real nice too."

"Please go!" I said sharply.

Higgins was coming into the room. "Well, Florri, I thought I recognized your dulcet tones. I hope you haven't said anything to this vulture, Miss Lockwood."

"Oh, Higgins, have a heart!"

Higgins grinned. "Out!"

"You be careful," the reporter warned him, "or I'll tell Jack Anderson that you were involved in Watergate."

Higgins grinned as he escorted the reporter to the door, so I gathered that they were old friends or old antagonists who knew each other well.

"Miss Lockwood," Higgins said then, "first Mrs. Garland, then Miss Winston, now Mr. Adams."

"What happened to Hart? Was he strangled too?"

"No, his head was smashed with a heavy granite paperweight. Someone wants something badly enough to kill for it, to kill and kill. For God's sake, Miss Lockwood, what is he looking for?"

When I could only shake my head, he made a little gesture of defeat and went out, only to poke his head back inside the door like a bird in a cuckoo clock and say, "Try harder, Miss Lockwood. I don't like to be an alarmist, but the life you save may be your own."

Once more I saw an ambulance draw up before the brownstone house and later Winnie's body was carried out. Still later a second ambulance double-parked, two men got out with a stretcher, and after a while they came out carrying Hart.

And then Roger came running up the stairs and hammered at my door, making me leap in my chair while my heart jumped and raced. He caught me in his arms and I could feel his heart thudding under my cheek. "I thought—I saw the ambulance and the police cars—I thought—oh, darling, I thought it was you!"

At last he released me and went to hang up his snowy coat in the bathroom and returned to exclaim contritely over the wet streaks left by the snow on my suit.

"It doesn't matter," I said impatiently. "It doesn't matter. Roger, Winnie was murdered last night, strangled with a scarf I had given her for Christmas, and her apartment was just torn apart. At least the living room was. Higgins wouldn't let me see the bedroom or Winnie, thank heaven. And Hart, Hart Adams, was nearly killed and the same thing happened to his apartment. But at least he's alive. They've taken him to the hospital and I don't know how bad his condition is, but apparently it's critical." I clutched at his sleeve. "What is happening here? What is it all about? Hope and Winnie and Hart! Oh, God, Roger, I'm frightened."

"There's one thing sure. You are going to marry me right away. We'll get our blood tests this afternoon and after that it will take three days. Until then I am staying here and afterwards I'll take you so far away that no one can touch you."

"You won't be taking her anywhere," Lieutenant Saxby said as he came into the room, followed by a sergeant whom I had not seen before. "Until we have cleared up two—maybe three—murders, Miss Lockwood will remain where we can keep in touch with her." Seeing Roger's rebellious expression, Saxby added, "Those are police orders, Mr. Mullen. At this point Miss Lockwood is an essential witness. She knew all the victims well. She was here in this building when the three attacks were made. I assure you it would do no good to attempt to take her away. It can't be done."

Roger surrendered to superior force but not with a good grace. "If anything happens to her—"

"Why should anything happen to her?"

"I leave it to you to find out, Lieutenant. You don't seem to have got far on the first murder. Nothing was done by the police to prevent a second or a third."

Saxby didn't like that. "And when it comes to Miss Lockwood's safety, I have no intention of standing back while something happens to her."

"We'll have her watched twenty-four hours a day until this case is cleared up, or at least until we know she is in no further danger."

I think Roger was as keenly aware as I was that the lieutenant's words were less a promise than a threat. Nonetheless Saxby made no objection to his sitting in while I was being questioned. "As long as you do not interfere or attempt to prompt Miss Lockwood."

"She has a right to a lawyer."

"Of course. But meanwhile—shall it be here or at the precinct?"

"Okay," Roger said, and he leaned back in his chair, arms folded, face schooled to expressionlessness.

It must have been two hours before Saxby gave up his questioning and by that time I was answering like a zombie. Fatigue and unaccustomed sleeping pills and shock, a whole series of shocks, had left me stupefied.

But even through the blur of confusion I remember that the focus had shifted from the murder of Hope to Hope's relations with her father, and her possible involvement in his affairs. It was the Phelps intrigues they were now investigating. Saxby inquired about the tapes which Winnie had mentioned and her being fired for looking into matters that did not concern her but vitally concerned Mr. Phelps.

He took me through my memories of the night before, the tramping around upstairs, the jingling of the crystals in my chandelier, which he could hear for himself as the detectives moved about Winnie's apartment.

"I was half asleep and I thought she was moving furniture."

"What time was this?"

I shook my head. "I have no idea. None at all. I had been deeply asleep—I took two sleeping pills—and was half awakened when something dropped upstairs, but even that was only a vague impression."

"Did Miss Winston have any enemies that you are aware of?"

"She was not a popular person. She had almost no friends at college except for Hope and me, and she had absolutely no social life. She just wasn't involved with many people outside her job, and I can't imagine any reason why her employer would kill her. Anyhow, that wouldn't account for Hope and Hart."

"Except that they were all involved—you were all involved—in one way and another with Marshall Phelps. I suppose it was just a stirring of the Christmas spirit that led you to invite Miss Winston and Mr. Adams to breakfast yesterday."

"Well, in a way it was. It was a spur of the moment thing. I hadn't planned it. But I had bought," I swallowed, "a scarf for Winnie and I thought—after all, it was the first time in five years we hadn't spent Christmas with Hope—so I asked her to join me for breakfast."

"And Mr. Adams?"

"I hadn't thought of asking him, but Winnie suggested it, knowing how crushed he was by Hope's murder, and it seemed like a good idea. Keep him from brooding all alone."

"What did you talk about?"

"Nothing in particular. Oh—"

"What have you just remembered, Miss Lockwood?"

"Winnie talked about Mr. Phelps and Hope and said some bitter things, which angered Hart, so it turned out to be rather unpleasant. She said she knew a lot she had never told and then she mentioned some tapes she had seen in the Phelps library, and finally Hart, who has always admired Mr. Phelps, got angry and left."

Sometime during that session my fingerprints were taken, over Roger's protests, but I agreed without demur. I've always thought every citizen should have his prints on record in case of accident.

Just before he left, Lieutenant Saxby got word from the hospital that Winnie had been dead for about nine hours and that Hart had suffered a concussion and had a deep cut in his scalp but there was no skull fracture and he would be able to return home in a few days. Men who had been checking, fingerprinting and photographing his apartment came up to report that it looked as though he had been sitting in his living room checking want ads when he was attacked. Apparently he had fallen beside his chair, as there was a big wet stain on the carpet from his bleeding scalp. His assailant must have left him for dead. The weapon, a paperweight, bore no prints.

"Oh, by the way," Saxby said casually as he was leaving the apartment, "Dr. Garland is being held by the police as a material witness in the death of his wife. Good afternoon, Miss Lockwood. Afternoon, Mullen. We're sure to be meeting soon."

And at last Roger, a grim and silent Roger, took me to lunch at the Algonquin, neither of us feeling in the mood for Christmas trees and skating on the Rockefeller Center rink. At the Algonquin Roger was known, and for a little while we almost had the illusion of living in a normal and pleasant world again among normal and pleasant people. The only flaw was the unobtrusive presence of a man in plain clothes who sat in the lobby where he could keep an eye on our table, which would have been unnerving if I had not been too exhausted to care.

On our way home Roger stopped to buy a bolt and a chain for my door. I reminded him that Winnie had had both and they had done little good.

"Well, of course," he said patiently, as though explaining the obvious to an exceptionally stupid child, "either she opened the door for someone she knew or the killer came up the fire escape. I hope your window on the fire escape is locked. I tell you, Sue, I hate like hell leaving you in this place."

"With an FBI man in the basement and a policeman at my door." I smiled reassuringly at him. "It will be all right, Roger. Nothing can happen to me."

Chapter 10

As I lay in the dark that night, the horrible events of the day crowded in on me. Winnie strangled with the scarf I had given her and which she had thought so pretty; Hart knocked out and nearly killed. The violence that had struck the brownstone house in the past twenty-four hours had almost dwarfed the murder of Hope. But why? Why? Why?

It seemed increasingly clear that the murders must have been committed by whoever was getting into the vacant apartment on the fourth floor and who could have gained entrance by way of the fire escape and unseen by the watchful Higgins. He might even be the same one who had got into the Marshall Phelps Fifth Avenue apartment the night he died. That two men could be so involved with the Phelps crimes seemed improbable.

But the most agonizing factor was the knowledge that the police were closing in on Larry. Now, at this very minute, he was probably sitting under a blinding light and being questioned by a number of men, all shouting questions at him. My ideas of police procedure continued to derive from late movies in spite of my own experience, which had not involved brutality or injustice.

In the dark my fear for Larry grew to unbearable proportions. I recalled that when a woman is murdered the police look first to her husband, but I remembered Larry's tender, protective manner as he walked down the aisle with Hope on his arm in her wedding dress with its floating, filmy veil. And I remembered, too, the hard look in the eyes that had swept over me without recognition.

Larry creeping into this house in pursuit of his wife, a noose in his hand? No, it was more than I could accept, perhaps because it was more than I could bear. And Larry strangling Winnie? Larry slugging Hart?

A heel. That was Roger's estimate of him. A heel. A kept man. The accusations, which had seemed ridiculous at the time, were different in the dark when I was tired and battered by the unspeakable shocks of the day. True, Larry had resigned from the job he loved. True, he had accepted the hospitality of the man he loathed. True, he had apparently had a bitter quarrel with Hope the night before she was killed, a quarrel during which she had threatened to sell the art gallery and leave him high and dry "unless he toed the mark."

Larry with his joyous laugh, his charm, his serene confidence in himself, his sunny confidence in his world. Larry behind bars for the rest of his life, his great talent rusting from disuse. Larry for one electric moment at the cocktail party, when we had turned to each other like a magnet to the north. I buried my face in my pillow, but not because I was crying; the pain was too deep for that.

Next morning, when I switched on the radio, and I had never before listened so intently to the news, I discovered that full play was being given to Larry being held as a material witness in the murder of his wife. When the reporters had exhausted the meager facts given them by the police, they fell back on the Marshall Phelps scandals and, with a wary eye for libel, attempted to link Larry with them. His hatred of his father-in-law, which he seemed to have proclaimed freely and frequently, was given more than a little attention. His stormy quarrel with Hope the night before she died was described in full in the highly colored words of her maid Frances. In fact, the arrest of Larry got so much play that the two attacks in the brownstone house the day before, although reported in full, were subordinated in interest.

One news item proved to be a great disappointment to avid readers who were now thirsty for sensation. Marshall Phelps had died a natural death from heart failure. While the attack might well have been brought about by a sudden physical or emotional shock, it could not, by any stretch of the imagination, be called murder.

That morning I became aware of the almost pathological interest in the brownstone house displayed by the public. There was a special article in the paper about the "house of horrors," as the imaginative reporter called it, with a tie-in to other houses whose "aura" had led to making them places of violence. After reading the first paragraph, I had thrown the thing away, but apparently there were more credulous readers.

Across the street from the house people had congregated to stare at the windows of the brownstone. What they expected to see, I can't imagine, as there was no one in the place except for Higgins and me and the policeman who had been left on guard and who was sitting in the hallway out of the cold. "The place where it happened." For some reason that is almost as satisfying to the ghoul as the sight of a potential suicide standing on a window ledge high above the ground. When I looked out, I was careful to keep well out of sight.

Impatient policemen on traffic duty kept calling "Move on! Keep moving!" That morning they were having their troubles. More uniformed men than usual had been assigned to the block and the reason was not hard to find. It was not the brownstone; it was the fact that the work of razing the buildings on my side of the street had begun. I wondered if this were not, in part, an attempt to drive out the tenants in the Phelps building because of the noise and confusion and the air choked with dust. The equipment had forced traffic into a single lane, providing a monumental traffic tie-up, and the noise was unspeakable.

One thing was sure, the minute, the very minute the police would allow me to leave, I was going to get out.

I did not know where I was going. Roger was determined to have me marry him at once, within the fewest number of days possible, but I kept, most dishonestly, shoving the decision into the back of my mind. I could not think of that now, not with everything so unsettled, so horrible. Not until I knew more about Larry's fate.

And then I heard a policeman's urgent whistle, saw him hold up traffic so that a taxi could draw in to the curb at the brownstone, and the driver got down to lend Hart a helping hand. Hart, with a bandage like a turban around his head, a black eye, a white-faced Hart, who shambled up the steps, grasping the railing, while the taxi driver assisted him, almost boosting him up. The policeman who had been left on guard came out to give a hand.

I raced down the stars. "Hart! Oh, Hart!"

Close up, he looked even worse. The taxi driver looked at the policeman with raised brows. "Okay to leave the guy with you?"

"Sure."

"I'm all right," Hart said unconvincingly when he had paid his fare and an ample tip for assistance. "Thanks very much." He looked at the policeman with puzzled surprise and then seemed to accept his presence without further curiosity.

"Okay, mister." The driver looked sharply from his battered passenger to the policeman to me with a "What goes on here?" expression. Then he went out to work his way into that sluggish line of traffic inching its way toward the corner, and held for what seemed like hours by red lights.

I took Hart's key and opened the door for him and he caught sight of his room. "Good God!" He let me take his overcoat and ease him into a chair. Then he looked at the policeman. "What on earth are you doing here?"

"I'm here to see that nothing more happens. You'll be okay, mister." He went out and I heard him speaking to another man in the hall, his replacement.

"What in the name of heaven is that in aid of?" Hart

demanded. "What a God-awful mess! Hope will be horrified when she sees what happened to her stuff." He broke off abruptly and bit his lips.

"Are you sure you should have come home so soon?"

"There's always a shortage of hospital beds and I can manage all right. The doctor just said to take it easy and he gave me some stuff for pain and something for fever, if either of them develops. What happened here, Sue?"

"What do you remember?" I countered.

He blinked. "I was checking want ads, sitting right here." He caught sight of the ugly dark stain on the light carpet. "Good God!"

"Well?"

"That's all! It looks as though the Battle of the Bulge had taken place in here. No, don't bother," he protested as I began to straighten the room.

"Oh, don't be silly! I have nothing else to do and I'd go mad just staying upstairs and brooding. Why don't you sit there quietly and be sensible and let me try to get this place into some kind of order? After all, you can't do it yourself and you can't live here while the apartment is in this shape."

He managed a grin. "Okay. More power to you, lady! Now suppose you tell me what happened."

At this point my nerves were in a state that made me jump at any sound, so hearing quick footsteps in the hall, I dropped the cushion I had picked up and stood listening intently. Then I heard the policeman challenge, "Where do you think you are going?"

"Second floor. Miss Lockwood. I'm her fiancé."

"Roger!" I opened the door and beckoned. "Come on down, will you? You can help me get this place straightened up."

Roger came running down the stairs, looked in the room and said, as Hart had done, "Good God!"

"The victim," I said, "is Hart Adams. And this is Roger Mullen." Hart's face brightened. He achieved a real smile.

"So you are the lucky guy Sue is going to marry!"

He held out his hand but wisely he did not attempt to get out of his chair.

"Quite a little home away from home you have here," Roger said, surveying the shambles. "What were you hiding, man? The Kohinoor?"

"I wish I knew. What on earth anyone could imagine I had that was of any value, anything worth tearing this place apart and slugging me——"

"And strangling Winnie," I said. There was no point in trying to soften it.

"Winnie!" Hart's jaw dropped. His hands tightened on the arms of his chair. "You aren't serious, are you, Sue?"

"Do you think I could joke about a thing like that? She was strangled with that scarf I gave her for Christmas and her apartment looks like this."

"Winnie!"

Roger lifted out of my hands the chair I was attempting to raise. Leaving Hart to digest the news of Winnie's murder, Roger and I straightened the living room and then, after a discouraged look at the bedroom, remade the bed and picked up the stuff that had been dumped on the floor from bureau drawers. We worked in almost complete silence.

It must have taken us an hour to get the place in shape—an hour during which Hart never spoke at all, sunk deep in his thoughts or in shock. I didn't know which. I did not attempt to question him. At last when we had done all we could, I looked in his refrigerator but found nothing of promise in the way of food. I came back to touch his hand and was startled to find it burning hot.

"You have a fever."

"The doctor said I might run one and he gave me some stuff to take. It's in a pocket of my overcoat." He did not seem interested.

Roger found the bottle, read the instructions, and brought it back with a spoon and a glass of water.

"I'm going up to get some stuff for lunch," I said, "and I'll cook it down here. Then you'd better lie down and get as much rest as you can. You've had a bad knock, Hart, worse than you realize. Don't try to overtax yourself yet."

He sat unmoving. "Thanks a lot, Sue. I'm not hungry. I think that fever has made me rather dopey. I'll lie down for a while."

"That's the idea," Roger approved. "You know Sue's number? Okay, call if you want anything and I'll come down. No trouble at all."

"How bad is it, Hart?" I asked.

"According to the doctor I have a concussion and a bad gash in my head, lavishly adorned with stitches. Beautiful stitches, regular works of art, I understand. I can't imagine what the guy hit me with. It bled a lot, of course. Scalp wounds do."

"It was a heavy granite paperweight," I told him.

"Sure you'll be all right?" Roger asked. "Shall I ask the cop to keep an eye on you?"

"Good God, no! I don't need a baby sitter. Anyhow, since Hope's death I don't care much what happens to me. There's no point in anything. I realized that when I was going over the want ads, looking for a new kind of life. It just doesn't matter any more. Excuse the bathos."

Roger made an uncomfortable sound, finding nothing adequate to say. I found I couldn't say, "In time you'll get over it," because that kind of statement never convinced anyone and it just infuriates people.

"It's a queer thing," Hart went on, almost as though he were talking to himself and not to us, "that I'd have given anything to marry Hope. Anything. And she fell for Larry." His fever-bright eyes narrowed as he looked at me. "What was it about Larry? You knew him, Sue. Hope couldn't see anyone else. At least in the beginning when everything was smooth. She couldn't see me at all. Her father—liked me. He wanted us to marry. Well, that doesn't matter any more. Nothing matters. But Larry never really loved her. Oh, he was kind enough in a lordly sort of way, but she didn't—matter to him. I doubt if even her death matters to the egotistical bastard."

"It matters," I told him dully. "Larry is being held as a material witness in Hope's murder. Apparently he was arrested a couple of days ago. I don't know why the police held up the story."

The change in Hart's face frightened me. "Larry? Larry! God! The murdering devil! If I could get my hands on him—"

In alarm I looked at Roger, who said dryly, "If you got your hands on him, he could push you over on your face as if you were a baby. You haven't the strength of a sick cat, Adams."

"For heaven's sake, calm down, Hart," I exclaimed. "You're only upsetting yourself."

"Upsetting myself." He laughed, his voice too high.

"Roger, can you get him to bed? While you are helping him undress, I'll call a doctor."

"I don't want to go to bed," Hart said with the unreason of a sick man.

"Relax and enjoy it," Roger advised him, and Hart managed a faint grin. "Oh, I'll come quietly." But he did not attempt to get out of the easy chair, ignoring the insistent pressure of Roger's hand on his arm. "Sue, why in hell was Winnie killed? What did she have? What did she know? Someone is searching for something important enough to kill for. But Winnie herself wasn't important. Could she have stolen anything from Hope or Mr. Phelps?"

De mortuis and all that, but this was murder. "She did take things," I admitted. "You remember that horseshoe brooch set with diamonds. Hope never gave that to her."

"That's what I suspected, but I didn't pay too much attention to it. In that white dress you sort of held the attention, Sue."

"And there was the gold compact." I told him how the policeman had prevented Winnie from picking it up when it had spilled out of Hope's big handbag.

"Hope was wonderfully generous to her," Hart said, "but I don't think she ever really trusted her."

"The time Hope came here to see me she said I was the one human being she trusted." I wanted to bite back the thoughtless words, realizing how they must hurt Hart.

"I wouldn't be surprised. You're rather a nice girl, Sue." Hart turned to Roger. "There's one sure thing, Mullen. The way things are I couldn't handle anyone with unfriendly ideas. I don't want Sue to stay here. She ought to get out. It's not safe. What with Hope and Winnie and then this damned attack on me—it's as though we had a maniac around here. Get your girl out, Mullen. That's my advice."

"I intend to," Roger said grimly, and after Hart had promised that he would call if he needed anything, he followed me upstairs to my apartment, while the policeman looked up from the paperback he was reading without attempting to stop us.

"I didn't tell Hart," I said when Roger had closed the door, "that the police won't let me leave. In his condition he'd just worry, and there's no sense in upsetting him any more."

"He is right, you know. You aren't safe here."

"With a bodyguard outside the door? I don't think Hart quite took that in."

"I still don't like any part of this."

"It's no use, Roger. The police won't let us get married yet."

"And that," Roger said dryly, "is fine with you, isn't it? I've noticed the way you've tried to curb your ardent desire to be my wife. Do we have to wait until this guy Garland is indicted for murder in the first degree?"

Roger's bitter words left an awkward silence behind them, a silence which he would not and I could not break. I prepared a soup and sandwich lunch which we barely tasted, and then Roger went down to help Hart undress and get him to bed, a task which eventually involved calling for additional assistance from

131

the policeman, as Hart was now so groggy he was unable to help himself.

"That guy really walked into something," I heard the policeman say when Roger came out of the hall. "They shouldn't have let him out of the hospital in his condition." He added reassuringly, "I'll keep an eye on him."

"And on Miss Lockwood."

"That," and I heard the policeman laugh, "will be a pleasure. Don't worry, mister. She's in good hands and nothing can happen to her."

Chapter 11

Next day the thing happened. I had gone back to modeling winter cruise outfits, though my shoes were caked with snow when I reached the store where the Christmas decorations, still as fresh as ever, nevertheless had begun to look faded and tarnished because their function was over.

Toward the end of an exhausting day the department head came into the dressing room where I was being helped into a stunning white evening dress. "Very nice," she said approvingly. "I had you in mind when I bought that model. In spite of the price, and it retails for six hundred and fifty dollars, it's going to be a smash hit. And here," and she handed me an envelope with a smile, "with the compliments of the management." It was the bonus she had promised me and considerably exceeded my hopes. She laughed when she saw my expression. "Now your feet won't ache so much," and she returned to her office.

Perhaps it was the state of euphoria into which that bonus check had plunged me, because it provided the rarest thing in my life—financial independence even for a short time, that made everything seem brighter when I came home that evening. Early December darkness had fallen over the city and for the first time in almost a week the sky was clear, the snow had stopped falling, and the air crackled with cold, nipping at nose and cheeks and fingers. What had been slush in the gutters that morning was now a film of ice that made walking treacherous. Building lights gleamed brightly.

After the perfumed but stale warmth of the store this frosty air was invigorating and I drew in long breaths.

I wondered how Larry felt about winter. Was he a winter or a summer man or a man for all seasons? We had known so little about each other, we had had so little time. And where he was he could not draw this frosty air into his lungs; he could not see the lights twinkling in windows and transforming Manhattan into a thing of beauty.

It was because I was thinking so intently about Larry that I did not notice, when I entered the brownstone and looked in my mailbox—a telephone bill and an invitation to the wedding of a girl whose name I only faintly recalled and whose face was a blank—that the policeman had been withdrawn.

In a hurry to change wet shoes and stockings, I went swiftly up the stairs and then had to fumble in my handbag for the key which, as usual, had slipped to the bottom. I neither saw nor heard anything. I unlocked the door, went into the apartment, and switched on the light. Then I felt the gun at my back and heard the whisper, "Quiet! Keep moving! Not a sound, sister, until I get the door closed. This gun is loaded, it's not a toy; in fact, I don't play games."

As I made an instinctive gesture, the whisper warned me, "Don't turn around. Do what you're told and you may come out of this all right. Where is it?"

"What?"

"Don't give me that. If you value your life, tell me what you've done with it."

It wouldn't matter. I knew that. Hope had not lived. Winnie had not lived. Hart had so nearly not lived.

"I don't have anything. I don't know why Hope and Winnie were killed. I swear I don't know. I honestly don't."

"So you want it the hard way." His manner changed. "Take off your coat."

Dazed, I remained standing where I was, my handbag dropping on the carpet.

"Take off your coat! Or do you want me to do it for you?"

I unfastened my coat then with numb fingers and he dragged it back over my arms and shoulders and tossed it on a chair. As he struggled with it, I turned my head swiftly and got a look at him. He wore a bright red wig, a long black beard and a monstrous artificial nose like that of Punch.

The scream that gathered in my throat was cut off when he turned me around, my back to him, one of his arms around me, holding me against him, though there was nothing amorous in that embrace. With the other hand he shoved up the sleeve of my wool dress. Now both hands were holding me and I could feel the needle plunge into my arm. Again, before I could scream, a hand covered my mouth.

I remember slumping against him and beginning to fall. I seemed to fall a long way, right down to the bottom of a dark tunnel, a very dark tunnel.

II

The tunnel was cold. It was also hard. Then someone was yelling, someone was shaking me, someone was shouting, "Sue! Sue! Damn it, don't stand there. Get a doctor. She's alive but she's been doped. Sue, wake up, darling; wake up."

"Lemme lone."

And someone laughed.

Then I heard Roger cursing again. "I want those pictures." There was a hard tone in his voice I had never heard before. "You aren't to have them."

"Take it easy, mister. These pictures are for the police. Nothing else. Your girl will be all right, I tell you. She just took a bigger dose than she could cope with."

"Damn it to hell," Roger raged, "she isn't a dope addict. She's never even smoked a marijuana cigarette in her life. Will you get a doctor or won't you?"

"Ambulance on its way. Hey, don't touch anything."

"I'm not going to leave her like that, providing a field day for you bastards. How would you like it if she were your wife?" And then I felt something soft and warm over me.

With the help of a young intern in a white jacket I came up out of the darkness into blinding light. After being horribly nauseated for a few minutes, I began to feel better except for an uneasy stomach and a confused head.

"Where did you get it?" the intern asked when I could see him clearly.

"Get what? I told him I didn't have anything. I told him and told him but he didn't believe me."

"Why was that?" This was Lieutenant Saxby's voice. I saw then, in bewilderment, that I was lying on my bed, covered by a blanket, and my little room was crowded with men in uniform and plain clothes, the white-jacketed intern with a stethoscope hanging around his neck, and Roger, grim-faced and watchful.

"Who was he?" Saxby asked.

"I don't know."

"What happened?"

I told him as accurately as I could. "And then I felt the needle in my arm."

"Can you describe him?"

"I got only one look while he was pulling off my coat. He wore a red wig and a long black beard and a monstrous artificial nose, the kind people wear at costume parties or on April Fool's Day."

There was an abrupt silence in the room.

"Well, well," Saxby said gently, and I knew he had not believed a word. "Well, well, what kind of voice?"

"He whispered."

Saxby laughed outright. "You got that description, boys? We're going to have quite a time finding this character."

"Are you implying that Miss Lockwood is lying to you?" Roger demanded grittily.

"Well"—Saxby let the amusement show through—

"if you can believe that story, you can believe anything."

"Then where," Roger demanded, "is the policeman who was supposed to be guarding Miss Lockwood? Where is your efficient FBI agent who never lets anyone get by him?"

That was one question to be answered immediately. There was a clatter of feet on the stairs and Higgins burst into my bedroom followed by the policeman who had been left on guard.

"Hey," Higgins exclaimed, "what goes on? Has Miss Lockwood been hurt?"

"Very useful guys, the two of you," Saxby said. "Mr. Mullen called to see Miss Lockwood and when she didn't answer, he walked in. The door was unlocked. Usual signs of ransacking. But the unusual thing was Miss Lockwood herself." He chuckled. "She took too much—" he corrected himself hastily—"she was given too much of some narcotic. She claims she was attacked by a guy wearing a red wig, a long black beard, and an artificial nose. He whispered."

"And why," Roger asked, his voice dangerously calm, "would she concoct such a story and dope herself, as you seem to be suggesting?"

"Somebody," Saxby said, "wants something bad. Very bad. Someone got into the Phelps library the night the guy died and ransacked it. Someone killed Mrs. Garland. It looked like we could throw all the blame on Lawrence Garland and then—surprise, surprise!—just when we have him safely under hatches, both Miss Winston and Adams are attacked. So we have to let Garland go."

In my enormous relief at knowing Larry was free I missed the next few words.

"... so with all the suspects out of the way Miss Lockwood had to stage the attack on herself to show she's in the clear. But what the hell led to all this mayhem?" he went on explosively.

"I can tell you that." Higgins's voice was high with excitement.

"I'll say so," the policeman corroborated him.

"Well?" Saxby's manner was not encouraging.

"There's a cache of money in hundred-dollar bills secreted in the chimney of the fireplace on the fourth floor. The stuff is behind some movable bricks. We didn't try to count it and we probably haven't found half of it. We just took a look—man!"

"And where did that come from?"

"Oh, it's Phelps's hoard, of course. It had to be somewhere. The guy had to pay for the way he lived. That's why he held onto this house and wanted his daughter's friends here, a cover for her to go back and forth and pick up money when it was needed. The department has known all along that Phelps was using this house for something, and now we know what it was."

There was a general and spontaneous movement toward the door and the irresistible lodestone of treasure. It was Higgins himself, even in that moment of triumph, who turned back to me. "This guy who attacked you—what did he want?"

"I've already told the police and they don't believe a word of it."

"Tell me anyhow."

"He just asked me where it was."

"And you hadn't the slightest idea what he meant?"

"Not the slightest. I knew he was going to kill me the way he killed Hope and Winnie. He had a gun and he said it was loaded, he didn't play games."

"What were you doing up on the fourth floor the day I caught you there?" Higgins asked abruptly.

"I told you the truth. I didn't like the idea of an intruder in the building, especially after what had happened to Hope. I wanted to make sure the place was locked up."

"And you thought this peculiar intruder of yours this afternoon intended to kill you?"

"I was sure of it."

"And yet all he actually did was to dope you, just enough to put you out—nothing lethal. Odd, isn't it?

And by the way, the footprints on the fourth floor were made by a woman's shoes."

I don't know why they didn't arrest me then and there. When I made no reply, he led the way up to the fourth floor, followed by the rest of the men, so they could examine the hoard of money, photograph and fingerprint and finally have it removed in an armored truck whose arrival, I learned later, caused a tremendous commotion on the street where, in spite of the nipping cold, onlookers had been attracted by the sirens, police car, and ambulance, which, to their disappointment, left without a body. This time the brownstone house had really paid off for its faithful watchers, though it was to be several days before the story of the discovery of the hoard was made public.

At last—it must have been nearly ten o'clock by then—everyone but Roger had left my apartment, which was a mess, with drawers overturned, coffee and flour and sugar canisters emptied on the kitchen floor, couch cushions slashed, the bedroom almost torn apart.

While Roger tried to straighten the living room, I dressed somewhat shakily and went into the kitchen to get some dinner, as I'd had nothing since breakfast but a drugstore sandwich and a carton of tepid coffee with too much cream. One look at the place and I revolted.

"I can't. I simply can't face it. Not tonight."

"We're going out to eat," Roger said firmly.

"With that crowd out there staring?"

"Let them stare!"

So, with a brief word to one of the policemen who cluttered the stairs—I might as well have been living at the precinct—he took me out into the cold, bracing air. There was a general move forward from the waiting throng and I shrank back, but Roger's hand tightened on my arm and the policeman who was restraining the crowd called, "Move on there! Keep moving!" He let Roger and me get through, though one woman managed to rip a button off my coat.

By luck there was a taxi cruising near the corner and

Roger hailed it. We had dinner at the Plaza. At first Roger said, "No, we aren't going to talk about it!" But when I had had a chilled martini and let him order a second one, I said, "I told the police the exact truth, Roger; just the way it happened."

"I know you did." He smiled at me. "You're a tiresome girl, Sue, always getting yourself into difficulties, but you are as truthful a person as I have ever known. So when you came out with that unbelievable story—" He broke off, as though listening to his own words. "Why, of course," he said softly, reaching for his second martini, "of course. No one was supposed to believe it. That was the whole point. You've been set up as the patsy, my child, with as lousy and incredible an alibi as anyone ever tried to sell to the police."

"But what happened after I was doped? I simply blacked out and I don't remember anything but being cold and lying on something hard and then I heard your voice and someone gave me a blanket." When I saw his expression, I tried to speak lightly. "I guess it's pretty bad."

"I'm afraid so."

"Wait until I've had my soup and then I'll be better able to take this."

So we drank turtle soup and I crumbled a cracker on my butter plate and took a long, fortifying breath. "You can fire when ready."

"Brace yourself, darling. You're going to hate this. It wasn't enough to dope you and let you have one look at that preposterous disguise. He stripped you and put you naked in your bathtub."

Chapter 12

NAKED MODEL FOUND IN BATHTUB

That was the delightful headline in the morning papers. The word *model* seems to excite some of the strangest reactions; although I spent most of my days weighted down with luxurious furs or wearing sports outfits, it was apparent to the public that I was a woman who earned her living by taking off her clothes rather than by putting them on.

No one could say outright that I had lied about my experience, but no one made any claim that I had been a victim. There was simply a straight-faced account of my mysterious bandit, and the description lost nothing in the telling. The model had been stripped naked and deposited in a bathtub where she was found by her fiancé, Roger Mullen, author of *Travels with Rosinante* and *A Bewildered Look at Taiwan*.

Undoubtedly the story about the naked model would have been even worse if it had not been submerged by the story of the discovery of Marshall Phelps's cache, or the cache alleged, assumed, etc., to be his. The amount was now estimated at about a quarter of a million dollars. All in all, the press was having a field day. The television boys weren't so happy. The fact that they weren't permitted to show pictures of me as I had been found was frustrating.

At half-past nine the department head telephoned to express her regret that the store would have to accept my resignation because of the unfortunate publicity to which I had been subjected. She was grateful that, so far, I had not involved the good name of the store.

I managed to laugh at that. "People don't want to know that I dress for a living," I told her.

"Well," she said briskly, "I'm glad at least that you can laugh at the whole distasteful business."

She had no sooner hung up than Hart called. "What happened to you, Sue? I just heard the story on the news, but it sounds so improbable—"

"Where were you yesterday from five to ten when all this was going on? The house was lousy with policemen."

"I guess I just slept through it," he said in chagrin. "That painkiller works like a sleeping pill. Were you hurt?"

"Just humiliated. And discredited. That, of course, is what he wanted; not to hurt me, just to discredit me. Why I am still out of jail, I can't imagine."

"What did this guy want of you? I can't figure this one out."

"I don't know, Hart. He asked, 'Where is it?' Oh, of course, you haven't heard yet, have you? Higgins and the policeman who was supposed to be guarding me were in that fourth-floor apartment, taking it apart inch by inch, and they found Marshall Phelps's hoard, at least that's what they think it is."

"Oh, yes, I heard that. Incredible, isn't it? You know I'd have sworn Phelps was as straight as any man who ever lived."

"And that must be why Hope came here with that big handbag. She wanted to get some money."

"You mean that Hope knew?" He was shaken by that.

"She must have known, Hart," I said gently. "You know how close a bond there always was between her and her father."

"So the two deaths and the attacks on you and me were just to find that money!"

I laughed at that. "A lot of people would think a quarter of a million dollars—dear God, the chimney must have been papered with the stuff!—would be worth a risk. Even a life."

"I suppose so. Well, take care of yourself, Sue. Damn it, why didn't Mullen follow my advice and get you out of here before anything happened?"

"He couldn't. The police won't let me go; that is, unless they drag me off to jail, which I rather expect to happen at any minute."

"Good God! Well, call me if you want me. I'm in a lot better shape this morning. That sleep seems to have fixed me up. I'll be out for an hour or so later this afternoon when I have to go to the hospital to have this cut in my head dressed. Otherwise, I'm at your disposal."

When the phone rang again, I nearly dropped it. It was Larry's voice and I sat staring at the telephone, not believing it.

"Sue?"

"Yes, Larry."

"I just heard the news—about you, I mean. It's a rotten thing to happen. Are you all right?"

At the same moment I asked, "Are you all right?" and it was as though time had rolled back to that magical day in spring and nothing had happened in between to separate us.

"Look, Sue, there's one thing I've got to make you believe. I didn't kill Hope. I never touched her. That last week I hated her guts. Between them she and her father had cheated me of everything in life I valued: you and my job and my faith in basic human dignity and decency. I believed her in the beginning, especially after your letter, which smashed things for us; and on top of that she told me you had offered to step out of the picture in exchange for a rent-free apartment, completely furnished, and ten thousand dollars in cash. And, like a fatuous idiot, I was flattered that she really loved me and needed me, especially since she was a pathetic case with a bad heart and all that."

He laughed without amusement. "The world's worst chump, that's me! Twice Hope had, and I quote, heart attacks. One was when I balked at moving into her father's apartment; the other was when Winnie the Pooh told her that she had seen me with a gorgeous blonde. She, by the way, is a cousin of mine and, for once, the description fits. Well, a couple of weeks ago I went to Hope's doctor for a routine check and found out that her heart was as sound as a bell. How she must have laughed at the gullible fool she married!"

"Larry!" I could not endure the fury, the bitter humiliation in his voice. "Stop! You can't say things like that about your wife!"

"I wouldn't to anyone but you. I hated her, but I swear I never touched her. I just intended to walk out and stay out, especially after I saw you at that party, looking lovelier than ever, so alive, so radiant." There was a cry of longing in his voice and, in spite of everything, my public humiliation and the suspicions of the police against me, I was happier than I had ever been in my life.

"I've got to see you, Sue."

"You can't."

"Why not?"

"Not because I don't want to see you," I answered the question in his voice, "but because the police are building a case against me. Apparently they think I was responsible for Hope's death and Winnie's and for the attempt to kill Hart and that I staged that attack on myself as a cover. They seem to think I was looking for the money that was found here. You heard about it?"

"Yes. Incredible, isn't it? I thought Phelps was one of the world's lousiest guys, but that sort of thing, concealing money to falsify income taxes—it just never occurred to me. But why are you supposed to have turned into this ruthless killer?"

"There are a lot of reasons. You are the primary one."

"I am!" He was startled.

"Oh, God! I forgot this apartment is bugged."

"Oh!" After a pause he said, "Look here, Sue. I've got to see you. Got to. We simply have to talk. Appar-

144

ently I can't go there without getting you in more trouble. Can you manage to leave the house without being followed and meet me—" There was a pause while he thought. "There's a movie theater on Third Avenue just a few blocks from where you live."

"I know the one." I had spent a lot of lonely evenings there.

"Meet me in the lobby. Buy your own ticket. Come at four or as close to it as you can. I'll wait for you. There's never much of an audience at that time of day, and anyhow they are showing a documentary that isn't exactly piling them in. Can you do that?"

"I don't know."

"Will you try?"

"Yes."

It was then that the siege began. It started with men at the door wanting to talk to me. When I discovered that they were from the news media, I shouted, "No comment," closing, bolting, and locking the door. "Go away," I called through the panels when they remained where they were, "or I'll have the policemen remove you."

One of them told me that the cop had been taken off duty. Obviously the police believed there was no need to guard me. I tried Higgins's number and his phone rang for a long time without an answer. He must be making a report to his superiors or else his task here was over. I thought of calling Hart and then abandoned the idea. He had no authority to send the reporters away, but an idea began to take shape in my mind.

Then the phone calls started. Every newspaper and everyone I knew in town seemed to be trying to reach me. After the fourth call I left the phone unanswered, though the persistent ringing got on my nerves, that and the sound of electric drills, the creaking of cranes, the throbbing of heavy equipment as the building down the street was being demolished.

As the phone continued to make its impertinent demands, I was grateful that Larry had reached me before the bombardment began. To have missed him by so slight a margin! Larry! I hadn't known happiness could be like that. There would be trouble ahead. Bad trouble, probably. But in the end it would simply have to be all right.

After lunch I began to make plans for meeting Larry. Of course if the policeman had returned to his post I would be followed, which would spoil everything. That was a risk neither Larry nor I could afford to take. And there were still watchers outside the house, staring open-mouthed at the blank windows of the brownstone.

An additional risk was the fact that, though the press had not been furnished with pictures of me naked in the bathtub, they had run a cabinet photograph which Winnie had kept in her living room and which, apparently, an enterprising reporter had scooped up. It had been reproduced in the papers and on television and, as it was an excellent likeness, it was quite possible that I might be recognized.

I hunted through my wardrobe and pulled out a white summer dress which was severely plain. I had no white stockings but out of a linen napkin I fashioned a nurse's cap. Regretfully I discarded my warm winter coat and replaced it by an unlined navy blue cape, totally inadequate for winter weather, but it did give the effect of a nurse's cape, particularly when worn with the jaunty white cap. I dared not telephone Hart because of the bugging—what a fool I had been to forget it when Larry called! The sound of his voice had driven everything else out of my mind.

I waited, my door slightly ajar—thank heaven, the reporters had given up in disgust. Anyhow they must have found the hall too chilly for loitering, now that Higgins was not taking care of the furnace. When I saw Hart's door open, I was out of my apartment like a shot and running down the stairs. I clutched at his arm. He started and then stared at me in bewilderment.

"Sue! What's this in aid of?"

"I'm the nurse escorting you to the hospital."

"But I don't need—" Then he grinned. "And just what do you think you are doing?"

I wanted to tell him the truth but I didn't dare. "I'm going to meet Roger and I don't want to make it a public affair. If you can take me in your taxi and drop me somewhere—anywhere, away from the house and that mob of gaping idiots, it would be fine."

"Will do. Hey, you'd better take my arm and act solicitous, hadn't you? Wait a minute." He went back to his apartment and returned with a pair of amber glasses. "Put them on. They'll help."

I opened the door and took his arm. Obligingly he played up, groping for the railing. Heaven knows he looked bad enough with that black eye and the turban around his head. We went down slowly. Someone took pictures of us during that descent. Automatically Hart stepped back so I could enter the taxi he had ordered ahead of him and I had to give him a poke before he remembered and got into the cab first.

He gave the addresss of the hospital in an unexpectedly carrying voice—he had really got into the spirit of the thing—and then leaned back with the listlessness of an exhausted man.

"This street sure is a mess," the taxi driver grumbled. "No wonder you couldn't pick up a cruising cab near here. That's New York for you. Put up a building and then tear it down in ten years. Planned obsolescence they call it." Then he seemed to do a double-take. "My God, that address where I picked you up—"

"Yes," Hart said, "that's where it happened."

"It sure looks like something happened to you! Who did it, do you know? That gal they found naked in the bathtub?" The driver chuckled. "A girl who'd do that to herself, make herself conspicuous-like, is up to no good. That's for sure."

"She certainly told an unconvincing story," Hart said, and grinned when I gave an indignant snort of protest.

At the corner of Lexington Avenue I exclaimed, "Oh, I forgot to pick up that stuff the doctor ordered,

Mr. Adams. Drop me here and I'll meet you at the hospital if you're sure you can manage alone."

"Oh, sure, sure. You run along."

"Maybe the driver will help you at the entrance," I suggested, and waited until the cab had moved on, holding the thin cape huddled close around me, shivering in the bitter air. Then I turned north for a block and went on to Third Avenue. There was no one at the box office when I got my ticket and the man inside the booth did not even look up as change rattled in the little trough and he pushed a ticket under the wicket.

In the dark lobby there was, to my relief, no usher, and as my eyes adjusted I could see that there was no need for one. There weren't more than three dozen people scattered through the theater, most of them elderly, as a sign outside advertised half-priced tickets for senior citizens.

And then I saw him. He had been leaning against the wall when I walked in and he had looked up and then looked away again when he saw the cap. I started towards him, my knees trembling.

"Sue!" He reached for my hands and stood crushing them so hard he hurt me. "Sue! I saw that cap and I thought—"

"A nurse." I was whispering too. "That's how I managed to get away, escorting Hart to the hospital."

"Did you tell him you were going to meet me?"

"No. Oh, Larry!"

He led me into the theater and found seats near the back. He reached for my hand again, as though needing the reassurance of the personal touch.

"You're cold."

"I didn't dare wear my warm coat. This cape seemed to be more in character."

We could not see each other's faces, just dim outlines, but it was Larry and he was there beside me. For the moment that was enough. Enough? It was all I asked of life.

There was something maddening about not being able to see his face, not being able to judge his mood because of the whisper. And when he did speak, it was not of me. Instead he said urgently, "What happened, Sue? What in God's name did Hope give you? It isn't safe for you to keep it."

From him I had not expected the question and I was obscurely disappointed. But then we were in an intolerable position, a dangerous position; this wasn't a normal world with normal people.

"She didn't give me anything. I don't know what someone is looking for if it isn't the money, I can't even imagine what it could be that would cause all this tragedy."

"You mean that Hope never gave you anything to keep for her?"

I shook my head and realized that he could not see me. "Nothing."

"What happened to her, Sue? You were there. The police are long on asking questions and short on answering them."

I told him about the discovery of Hope's body. He interrupted swiftly, "Then you found her?"

"No, Winnie did."

"Winnie," he said thoughtfully. "Go on. Details, please."

So I told him about Winnie's murder and the attack on Hart and then last night's attack on me. In every case, except for Hope, of course, the apartments had been ransacked.

"But that happened at the Phelps apartment too," Larry said. I noticed that he did not say *mine* or even *ours,* and that was a faint comfort. "At least it happened after Phelps died. The library and his bedroom had been searched pretty thoroughly."

"I don't understand it. You and Hope and Hart were there at the time and heard nothing?"

Larry released my hand as though there had been an implied doubt in my voice. "Odd of us, wasn't it?" There was hostility in his manner.

"Larry, I didn't mean that. You know I didn't. But

whoever was searching the Phelps apartment couldn't have known where the money was hidden."

"In my opinion," Larry said, still in that strained whisper, "it wasn't money that he was after. I think the discovery of the money came as a stunning surprise to everyone except for the FBI and the Treasury boys. No, what someone is looking for, must be looking for, is one of the tapes Phelps had made of his conversations with the people who visited him in that library of his. It was fairly papered with them, from all I can make out. They were hidden in the damnedest places: in what appeared to be bound books, at the base of a floor lamp, in a cigarette box. Not a man who trusted his fellows was our Phelps. Apparently he didn't even trust Hart, who was stunned when he learned about the way Phelps had had that room bugged. Lord, when you think of what that man was up to, the things he was involved in, there must be enough evidence there to blow up a third of the country. Not that the police or the FBI are talking about it. But one thing seems to be sure: somewhere there is an important tape that no one has yet discovered."

"Winnie knew about the tapes." And then because I couldn't wait any longer, "What about you, Larry?"

"I thought you'd seen that in the press. Hope and I had a big row, gloves off. She'd seen on television our meeting at that cocktail party. Of all the damnable luck! It was a dead giveaway, of course, and I didn't help matters by getting drunk that night. Anyhow, Hope accused us, you and me, of carrying on an affair. When I had convinced her that it wasn't true, she went into a song and dance about my meeting with my cousin Claire, who was in New York for a day and in trouble up to her pretty neck. She was running away from her husband, so I refused to say who she was or where she was for fear Hope would get the poor girl into more of a mess than she's already involved in.

"Well, in the course of this delightful conjugal meeting Hope said if I wasn't careful she'd sell the art gallery, leaving me high and dry, and I told her to go right ahead. Nothing I'd like better. I'd go back to teaching. And then she tried to stage a heart attack and I laughed. I'd talked to Dr. Partridge just a week before and I told her so.

"Did you ever see Hope angry? Not hot anger. Cold. All those months I had never realized that she had a cruel streak. She appeared so fragile, and her manner was gentle, aloof, detached. But once I saw her as she really was, I realized the kind of hell she had put Hart Adams through. He adored her but she asked him to act as my best man at our wedding and she insisted on his staying at the apartment. I think she got a kick out of watching him writhe. She never acted as much in love with me as she did when he was around.

"Well, after that happy encounter I decided that I wanted out. I'd had all I could take. Anyhow, I had seen you again and I had a reason for breaking away. Without you nothing made much sense. So I left the apartment, went to the gallery to close up, and then—" He paused and went on rather sheepishly, "I went on a bender. Sometime during the night I was eased out of a bar—no rough stuff, all done with kindness—and when the cold air hit me, I knew I'd gone in way over my head. I managed to get to a Turkish bath, where I was eventually found and picked up by the police.

"I was knocked flat, of course, when they told me about Hope's murder. They hammered at me with questions about her death, trying to prove that I was the only one with a motive for killing her. Our knock-down-and-drag-out fight had been overheard, of course, by Frances, who seems to live with her ear at a keyhole. They said I could not prove that I had not gone to the brownstone house but, on the other hand, they certainly could not prove I had. Though where I had been only God knows, for I certainly don't.

"Well, in the long run they decided to hold me as a material witness. They were sure I was guilty, but they hadn't enough proof. It wasn't until Winnie was killed that they figured I could hardly have done that while I was under their noses, so they released me. I'm supposed to be a free man, but I wouldn't bet a nickel that there isn't a plain-clothes man within range of us at this very minute. Oh, the hell with it!"

He put his arm around me and his left hand slid down my arm to my hand. "I love you, Sue. Even when I thought I hated you for walking out on me that way, I loved you. I'll love you forever." His cheek was pressed hard to mine and his hand tightened on mine and felt the ring.

"I seem to have spoken out of turn," he said, and he was a stranger, a hostile stranger sitting beside me in the dark. "I had no idea you were engaged. Whose ring is that?"

"He is Roger Mullen, with whom I have been working on a book, illustrating it. He gave me the ring as a protection in case the police tried to establish an emotional relationship between you and me. It was the gallant action of a loyal friend, Larry."

"He must also be well-to-do," Larry said pleasantly. "As I remember that loving letter you sent me, you are not interested in men without ambition, men who do not collect any moss as they go along. I trust this guy has plenty of moss."

I was so angry that the words came without my even having thought of them, "At least Roger doesn't expect his wife to support him."

Larry jerked on his overcoat and went out of the theater, leaving me alone.

Chapter 13

Dromedaries trudged along the sandy horizon like something out of a chapter of *Exodus,* so blurred that I could hardly make them out, and I wiped my cheeks with the backs of my hands impatiently. Larry was gone, gone forever this time, gone after we had exchanged unforgivable insults. He had asked me to meet him only to find out what had happened, what I knew or guessed, whether or not Hope had left anything with me.

The discovery of the money had surprised him but it had not greatly interested him, I thought. His most pressing interest was in what Hope might have given me or told me.

If Larry was to be believed, he had never heard of the tapes until after Phelps's death. If he was to be believed. Hart had been kept in a state of innocence from the beginning because it was only as a patently honest man that he could serve Phelps's purpose. Of course Hope had known, and Winnie, in her prowling, had discovered something.

I sat in the theater, staring unseeingly at the screen, dimly aware that a cultivated voice was explaining how the desert could be made to flower, to produce food, to support human life. At length I realized that I was chilled to the bone in that summer dress and unlined cape. The theater was not overheated for its scanty afternoon audience.

It was dark when I left and the wind cut through my inadequate clothing. I signaled a cruising taxi, started to give the address of the brownstone, and changed my mind, asking to be let off at the corner of Fifth Avenue. I could walk the rest of the way.

My street was a shambles where the building was being torn down, with a hastily erected fence to prevent passers-by from being hit by falling bricks or masonry. Tonight no one seemed to be watching the house but, as I came nearer, I saw a familiar figure going up the stoop. Roger. Ahead of me, in the narrow walkway for pedestrians, a woman had filled the whole space with a baby carriage, so I had to back up to the end of the path to let her pass. By the time the path was clear, Roger had disappeared. I stopped at my mailbox, which was jammed with letters. Apparently everyone who had ever known me was eaten up with curiosity to know what had happened. I stopped for a moment to riffle through the envelopes and then opened the inner door.

"Hello there," Hart was saying cheerfully, sounding much more like himself. "Where did you leave Sue?"

"Leave her?"

"Don't tell me the poor girl missed you after going to all that trouble to meet you!" Hart exclaimed in concern.

"You mean she isn't here?" Roger was startled.

"No, she isn't back yet. I was just coming down from her apartment. I wanted her to have a drink with me. But you come along anyhow. No use standing in this drafty hall. All I can give you is some whisky; I don't try to stock a cellar."

"Well, thanks."

"Roger!" I called.

He looked at the nurse's cape and cap, and he didn't ask any unnecessary questions. "You're freezing," he said abruptly. "Run up and get a hot shower and put on some warm clothes. I'll take advantage of Adams's offer of a drink and see you in thirty minutes. Okay?" Without giving me time to reply, he preceded Hart into his apartment. The latter took a long, thoughtful look at me, his brows arched in a silent question.

When Roger appeared, it was exactly thirty minutes

later. I was warm and dressed in a sweater and wool skirt, and I had managed to get my hair, tightly curled under the hot shower, into some kind of control.

"That's better." He smiled at me. "A lot better. For a moment I thought you were heading for a nice attack of pneumonia."

Mutely I pulled off the opal ring and offered it to him.

He made no move to take it. "Why, Sue? Why?"

"Because I've been making use of you—inexcusable, unforgivable use. That ring was my protection against the questions of the police and their suspicions, but I can't go on with it. That's not fair to you."

"Or to Larry," he suggested evenly.

"Or to Larry," I agreed. "Not that it matters to Larry at all. He isn't—interested. But I want to give back the ring and I want to tell you where I've been."

"You want to tell me because I know you've been with someone else instead of with me, isn't that it? You're telling me because Adams let the cat out of the bag."

I could feel the color burning in my cheeks, but I had deserved that. "All right. I lied to Hart. I didn't want to have to explain to him."

"You needn't explain to me, you know."

"I think I do. I owe you that." Roger made a faint grimace but no comment. "Larry called me this morning. He wanted to see me, and the only way I could manage it, without being recognized and followed, was to dress like a nurse and pretend to escort Hart to the hospital."

"Would it have mattered if you had been followed?"

"Well, of course it would! A meeting between Larry and me would just provide another motive for my killing Hope."

"Oh," he seemed to be interested in a mild way, "so you had a motive for killing Hope."

"Why, the money, of course."

"Of course. Stupid of me not to think of that. Look here, Sue, would you mind awfully if we sit down? I've been rushing around town all day trying to work out a travel schedule that will cover the Scandinavian countries in depth, and to arrange for the two of us to leave as soon as the police give you permission."

"But, Roger—" As he made a gesture, I sat down and he followed suit. Then he got up again. "I'll fix us some drinks. I'm already one ahead of you."

"Roger!" I sounded rather desperate. He was making it unexpectedly hard for me.

"Later," he said. "All in good time." I waited helplessly while he rattled ice and I heard the tinkle of glasses. When he came back, he brought a tray with a pitcher, two glasses, and a plate of crackers and cheese. "I forgot lunch." When he had poured the drinks, he spread a cracker with cheese, apparently giving the simple operation all his attention.

"Roger," I began again. He looked up, started to speak, and then smiled. "Go ahead, darling, with this soap-opera confession of yours. Don't you see by now that I don't give a damn about that guy you think you're in love with? If he'd been worth the powder to blow him to hell, he wouldn't have asked you to go to a surreptitious meeting, especially when the police are suspicious about the nature of the relationship between you and the motive it suggests for murder. When you get those blinders off, you'll know he's not worth all this trouble. But I must say that, on the whole, I'm glad you did see him. I think you've been skating on thin ice and this afternoon you broke through and got a cold bath. It's tough in a way but better in the long run. I'm more hopeful about my own prospects right now than I've ever been before."

He took the ring off the table and slid it back on my resisting hand. "Now, now, keep still," he advised me, and lightly kissed my fingers. He leaned back in his chair, the cocktail glass in his hand. "Okay, let's have it before you burst."

And somehow the confession that was to be so painful became absurd and I found myself laughing.

While I told him about that disappointing and disenchanting meeting in the darkened theater, of the whispered conversation, he listened without making a comment, now and then taking a meditative sip of his drink. When I had finished, the silence in the room went on and on. Finally he refilled our glasses and urged me to eat a cracker and cheese.

"It will take the edge off your appetite," he said when I refused, "and then you won't be so expensive to feed tonight," and again I laughed. Roger had very disarming ways.

While I nibbled the two crackers he spread for me, he sat tapping a thoughtful finger on the table. Then he said, "You know, this has been a queer setup, Sue. We've missed the boat somewhere. Everyone has missed the boat: the police, the FBI, and the guy who is looking for something and destroying everything and everyone who gets in his way. About the only satisfied people around are the Treasury boys with Phelps's cache of money."

He broke off thoughtfully to say, "Isn't it odd to find someone as hard-boiled as Phelps doing something as romantic as hiding a hoard of money behind bricks in a fireplace? As though he were imitating a cheap thriller, the way Hoover is said to have imitated the western movies he loved whenever he staged a raid and sent his men in with guns popping all over the place."

Roger got up to close the drapes. It was dark and he shut out the night and any watching eyes. "Let's go to the beginning and see if we can get a new slant on the whole business. The odd slant is no good. It's focused in the wrong direction. I can feel that in my bones."

For the first time since my disastrous meeting with Larry I was interested in something outside my own feelings. "But what is the beginning? Hope's murder?"

"No, it goes farther back, probably to Phelps's death."

"But he wasn't murdered. He died of a heart attack."

"All right, but what caused that heart attack? According to all reports, Phelps kept himself in fine condition physically."

"Yes, he did, daily exercise, massage, even boxing."

"So it took a hell of a shock to bring about a fatal heart attack."

As I started to speak, Roger said eagerly, "Wait, darling. I'm leading up to something in my own circuitous way; at least I hope I am. What has made the whole thing so confused is the multiplicity of Phelps's activities, as they have come to light, and the range of people involved in them, some directly, some peripherally. But it isn't actually as complex as it appears. Only a limited number of people had access to that library. The servants have all been eliminated by the police because they alibi each other, so we are left with the members of his family: Mrs. Garland, her husband, Adams, and the visitor—if there was a visitor—in the library at the time Phelps had his heart attack. Because, my darling, something that happened that night led to the death of Phelps and, later, to the murders of his daughter and the Winston woman."

"It's a nice theory," I admitted, "but I don't see that it throws a great blinding light on anything."

"Do you see any flaw in it?"

"Yes, but I don't know what it is."

"You disappoint me. There didn't need to be a stranger in the Phelps library that night. He might have been talking on the telephone and got the message that shocked him and brought about his death."

"What could be easier to prove?" I said enthusiastically. "Just ask the mysterious caller to come forward and declare himself and, naturally, he'll do it without hesitation."

"No lip from you, woman. And there is another way of proving it."

"And what is that?"

"The tape made of any telephone call. For my money that is what someone is looking for, what someone has to have. If Phelps had the place practically papered with

158

tapes, he must have had his telephone calls monitored too."

"It's a lovely theory. You assume a telephone call and a tape that recorded it; you just conjure them out of thin air."

"Out of recognition of what is probable."

"But you forget one thing, Roger, both the library and Mr. Phelps's room were searched, and the library door to the outer corridor was unlocked. So we can go beyond the immediate family."

There was understanding in the look Roger gave me, aware that, in spite of everything, I was determined to keep Larry in the clear. "The fact that the door was unlocked does not necessarily indicate the presence of an outsider. Actually your stranger is as theoretical as my telephone call. Besides," and Roger grinned, "it is much neater not to add to this cast of unsavory characters. Anyone discovering Phelps's unexpected death might have got into a panic, knowing what dynamite there was to be destroyed, what incriminating evidence had to be disposed of at once."

"So who searched the library and his bedroom?"

"My first candidate would be his daughter. Evidently he confided in her. She would be apt to know what evidence would be injurious to his reputation. Then there is her husband, your Larry, but, for my money, he'd as soon as not have Phelps's reputation blown sky-high. So we are left with Hart Adams."

"Oh, for heaven's sake!"

"I know. It's unlikely. But there you are."

I shook my head. "Hart does not know what is behind this or what someone is looking for. And, for heaven's sake, don't forget what happened to him."

"So we come back to Mrs. Garland. What I think happened is this: she knew where to look for the incriminating tape and she concealed it. Then, perhaps because she had been threatened, or for some other reason, she entrusted it to someone else. And that, I believe, accounts for the attacks on Miss Winston, Adams, and you."

"Well, Hart doesn't have it and if Winnie had it, she must have stolen it."

"When could she have done that?"

"The night before Hope was killed she asked Winnie to go to see her. She accused her of having sent an anonymous letter to the FBI about her father's activities and suggesting to the police that her father had been murdered. Winnie had also gone through her boss's files and found some incriminating evidence. While she was at the apartment she took Hope's diamond brooch, which she said later Hope had given her and then admitted that she had taken. She said that Hope owed her something. Hope was coming here to retrieve it when she was killed. When Winnie found her on the stairs—"

"Found her?"

"I suppose so. I heard a queer sound in the hall, a kind of choking sound, and a fall, and then, almost immediately afterwards, Winnie screamed. Like a fool she lied to the police and said she had just been coming in the building, but they could see, as well as I did, there was no snow on her coat. And when I pointed that out to her, she admitted she had been going out to avoid Hope and when she found her dead, she panicked and was afraid to say she had been in the building. But—Roger, I honestly don't believe she killed Hope. That noose meant premeditation. She couldn't have managed it. And then Hope's fall and Winnie's scream—not a full minute between them. Winnie must have caught at least a glimpse of the killer or heard something to suggest who it was."

Roger frowned. "According to your theory Hope came to retrieve the brooch and/or the tape from Winnie." He shook his head. "No, this doesn't make sense. The Winston woman obviously didn't have that tape or it would have been found during the search of the apartment. Adams didn't have it. So we come to you."

"Me!" The word was a squeak. My eyes must have been as big as an owl's, because Roger laughed. "I don't mean that you have or had the tape, stupid. I just mean that someone thinks you have it."

"Nice for me," I said dryly. "Especially now that the police have taken away my bodyguard."

"I don't think well on an empty stomach," Roger said. "Let's go out and blow away the cobwebs."

I balked. "People might recognize me."

"Let them. It builds a man's ego to go out with a beautiful woman."

"If they remember the headlines, they'll laugh."

"No," he said grimly, "they won't laugh."

So we went out, not to Sardi's, as he suggested, but to a big impersonal Italian restaurant filled with a crowd that was absorbed in its own affairs and paid little attention to us. Something about the cheerful atmosphere reminded me of the little Italian restaurant where Larry and I had talked away so many happy hours, and all of a sudden, like that dismal and vacillating lover of Dowson's, "I was desolate and sick of an old passion."

I sat crumbling a breadstick while Roger talked gaily and rather desperately, trying to bridge the gap between us. We were eating roast chicken when I found my brain functioning again. "Look here, Roger, this is rather grim, you know. Someone who seems to be on a killing spree believes that I have that tape. Otherwise there's no reason for that attack on me. And he's going to try it again. So what am I going to do?"

"I'm in this too, you know. We're going to find it first."

"No sooner said than done."

"I don't like sarcastic women. More Chianti? Come on, let me fill up your glass. Do you good. That's better. So what we've got to do is to put our heads together—a nice idea, anyhow—and find out where it is."

"But someone searched every inch of Winnie's apartment and Hart's and mine."

"I don't know whether it has occurred to you that the act of strangling a woman is apt to be rather a strain on the nerves. The guy must have been frantic to clear out as fast as he could. He must have slipped up somewhere and overlooked the tape."

"In other words, it must still be in Winnie's apartment."

"That's my guess. Find the tape and you'll find the murderer, or at least the reason for the murders. Then Sue and Roger, hand in hand, will wander happily off into the sunset." He broke off as he saw my face. After a long time he said, his voice remote, "Dessert?"

"Not tonight, thanks."

We walked home without attempting to talk.

Chapter 14

One thing was increasingly clear to me. Roger was the nicest person I had ever known, probably the nicest I would ever know, but I could not marry him. Logic, common sense, nothing had anything to do with it. Whether Larry loved me or not, whether he was guilty of any part of the crimes of the past week, had nothing to do with it. The bond between us, whatever it was, could not be snapped. Unhappiness with Larry would be better than happiness with any other man. Irrational? Of course. But too many women have been driven by the same compulsion for it to be strange.

I took off the opal ring for the last time and put it away in its little box. I did not think that Roger would insist again about returning it to me.

Next morning two more detectives came to question me. These were not like the questions I had been asked before. After a few minutes I realized that Higgins must have told them that the apartment was bugged and they had a record of what had happened there. Perhaps because I could not see the bug, whatever or wherever it was, I kept forgetting its existence. Certainly the night before when Roger and I had thrashed out the whole case, I had revealed everything I knew. And, more important, the police must have heard something when I was attacked.

They wanted me to repeat my description of the man. "I had only one glimpse of him," I explained, "and obviously he intended me to see that disguise. Otherwise it would make no sense at all. It was not the kind of thing he could afford to be seen in on the street. He must have put it on right outside my door. And his voice—just a whisper—" An idea occurred to me. "Oh, of course you must have heard that whisper, so you know I was not lying about it."

"We heard the whisper," the older of the two detectives admitted at length. After all, they owed me that. "And there was the sound of someone walking heavily through the apartment while it was being searched. I understand he pretty well tore the thing apart."

"That's for sure."

But they were off on another tack now. "Now that whisper—did it remind you of anyone?"

"One whisper sounds like another," I protested.

"Did it occur to you to wonder why this character whispered?"

"Afraid he'd be overheard, I suppose. What else?"

"Or afraid that you would recognize his voice."

"But that's preposterous. Nobody I know would have treated me like that. It was a cruel thing to do."

"We're dealing with a cruel boy, lady, in case the thought hadn't struck you. A strangler is not a pleasant character." The detective shifted his ground easily. "I understand you went to quite a lot of trouble to meet Dr. Garland yesterday."

"Then someone must have followed Larry," I said with conviction, "because no one could have followed me."

"Quite an interesting little talk the two of you had." Unexpectedly the detective smiled at me. "Don't look so sick, Miss Lockwood. If we are fairly sure about anything in this queer case it is that you are not involved in the deal, except as a victim. But you'd be playing it smart if you stayed clear of Garland for a while."

"He couldn't be involved in this thing. I know him so well."

"I suppose you know where he was when you were attacked."

"No, but—"

The detective gave me no opportunity to finish. Un-

164

expectedly he shifted his line of questioning. "What were you doing on the fourth floor when Higgins caught you up there?"

"Just what I said. Trying the door. Winnie had talked about someone walking overhead and Higgins admitted that there had been an intruder in the building. I didn't like it."

"The footprints in that vacant apartment weren't made by a man, Miss Lockwood. They were made by a woman."

"So Higgins said. But it must have been Hope. It had to be. She must have come here fairly often. I realize now that the day we met at the door she hadn't intended to see me. I startled her. And she knew the house well, and commented on a hole in the stair carpet as though she were familiar with it. If her father had money hidden here, she must have been able to get at it. That stands to reason."

I did not mention Roger's theory about the tape, which might or might not be hidden in Winnie's apartment, but I did suggest that it could not have been Winnie's footprints in the fourth-floor apartment. If she had got wind of that money, it certainly would not have been there for the police to find.

"Anyhow," I went on, thinking aloud, "I can't see how that much money could possibly be concealed behind a few bricks in a chimney. It simply isn't possible."

"Now that's where you are quite right, Miss Lockwood. Some bricks had been loosened and a space cleared behind them for ready cash, I suppose. But built into the chimney—and it's big enough for a man to stand upright—there is a safe."

"You mean Mr. Phelps had that made? But then the workmen would know and wonder about it."

"No, he wasn't the one who had it built. Higgins has done some research on this house. Back during the Second World War suspicions were aroused against what appeared to be a fine upstanding college professor. He was arrested as a German spy and this house— he owned it then—was just about taken apart at the seams. That's when the built-in safe was found in that very peculiar chimney.

"Well, the papers played up the story at the time, of course, and there was a lot of excitement about the hidden safe. But people forget. Each day's news pushes out that of the day before. Marshall Phelps traded on that. He bought the house and then was willing to wait, or perhaps at that time he had no pressing need for it. As long as no one questioned his integrity, it wasn't necessary for him to cover his steps. Now and then he would rent out one of the lower floors, but the whole thing was more trouble than it was worth, and for the most part the place was left vacant.

"Then when he needed a place to conceal his money, a place less likely to be detected than a safety deposit box, he turned to this house. You remember there was, not long ago, an attempt to discover which leading industrialists in this country were putting large amounts of money in numbered accounts in Swiss banks and he was afraid that the government officials would be more honest than they proved to be and carry out the exposure. He had his daughter persuade you to take an apartment here to provide her with an excuse for coming back and forth to the house when it was necessary to do so."

"So that's it!" I began to laugh. "After Watergate I thought nothing could ever shock me again, but this does."

"Oh, we get these stories now and then. The stranger-than-fiction kind. A lot of stuff that never gets into the news."

"You are sure now, aren't you, that there really was an intruder who doped me and searched this apartment?"

"Well, we like evidence, you know, but we've found some." He smiled. "There's one factor you've overlooked, isn't there? The hypodermic. You got that dose in your arm. The Doc says you wouldn't have had time to conceal the hypodermic before you passed out, and there was no hypodermic in this apartment. Our boys guarantee that."

"And the police have known this all along?" I asked indignantly.

"Not exactly. Anyhow," he went on, smiling, "this should cheer you up. Some kids over on Second Avenue were poking around in a garbage can and they found a red wig, a long black beard, and an artificial nose." As he saw my expression, his smile broadened. "They took the disguise home to play with and one of them jabbed his finger with the needle of a hypodermic, which had been wrapped up in the wig. So the mother, who fortunately believes those stories about calling the police, did so. Evidently that description of your intruder had made an impression on her, that and—"

"And the naked model found in a bathtub," I said in resignation.

At length the two men got up to leave. "Keep your door locked and make sure whom you let in," the lieutenant said in a cheering way as he took his departure. "Miss Winston seems to have had a trusting nature."

Or, and I remembered Roger's comment, she might have admitted someone she believed to be a friend.

The detective turned back. "And, if you'll take my advice, you will give Dr. Garland a wide berth. You know how people are; they add two and two—"

"And get five," I said.

"Well, quite often, you know, they come up with the right answer. It's not, after all, a difficult sum."

II

The police had hardly left the building before Hart came running up the stairs. He identified himself and I unfastened the bolt and the chain and let him in, feeling like the Prisoner of Chillon, except that the bolts were on my side.

"I'd have come sooner but I thought maybe you'd

rather I didn't bust in. I know you'd call me if anything—if you needed help."

"Thanks a lot, Hart." I collapsed in my chair and found that I was shaking. "They were really pleasant enough. It was just—" I realized that while I had thought I was perfectly calm and in full possession of myself, I was carefully ripping up one of my best handkerchiefs, a handkerchief, I remembered, that Hope had given me.

"What did they want this time? Yesterday when Mullen came, and it was obvious that you hadn't had a date with him, I was afraid that you were in some kind of trouble, or up to something."

"No, things are really brighter for me now than they were. The police know that there really was an intruder, that I didn't stage the attack myself. And, what's more, they found the disguise and the hypodermic with which I was drugged."

"What!" He was astounded, unbelieving. But when I had told him of the discovery made by the two little boys and how their mother had turned the evidence over to the police, he expelled a long breath of relief. "Well, that's good news!" He reached over and patted my hand. "Though how anyone could expect you to have had any part in that filthy business, I can't understand. He'd have to be nuts, and the police aren't nuts. Far from it."

His kind smile faded. "Look here, Sue. It's none of my business, I know that, but Mullen is a hell of a good guy and he's crazy about you. I wouldn't like to see him—" He noticed then that there was no opal ring on my left hand. "Don't do anything hasty. Don't do anything—foolish. I don't know what you think you are trying to prove, but leave it to Mullen, can't you? A good, straightforward, trustworthy guy."

I answered desperately, feeling on the defensive. "I know all that. I know just how good he is. I know it better than you do, but I can't help it."

"What is it, Sue?"

"It's Larry," I said helplessly.

"I—see. That's what I was afraid of."

"That's where I went yesterday. He called me. He—we—had to talk."

"You must be mad," Hart said roughly. He had never spoken to me like that before. I had never heard him speak like that to anyone before. "Stark, staring mad. You'd throw over a guy like Mullen for a rat like Larry Garland. All-conquering Larry, the lady's man." He added deliberately, "The lady-killer."

"That's a rotten thing to suggest, just because you were jealous of him."

"Jealous? Yes, I was. I saw him take away the only woman I ever loved, a woman he didn't care two hoots in hell about. Why he married her I don't know unless it was for that plush apartment and the art gallery."

"But the gallery belonged to Hope," I pointed out.

"Phelps wasn't a fool, especially where Hope was concerned. He wasn't going to let Garland have everything his own way. He told me when he bought the gallery it would give Hope a hold on the guy in case he ever wanted out."

The buzzer sounded. "That's the mailman with a package," I said.

"I'll get it for you. Don't go wandering around the halls unless you know who is there." Hart went down the stairs and in a few minutes he came up, an odd expression on his face. "Special delivery." He put the letter in my hand. Larry's return address was in the corner. Hart stood looking down at me. "So long, Sue," he said heavily. "Lock the door after me."

After he had gone, I shoved home the bolt and put on the chain and then turned to my letter. It began abruptly:

> Forgive me if you can. I don't know what got into me. The minute after I left the theater I knew what a fool I had been, but I wasn't man enough to swallow my pride and come back to tell you so. There's no point in calling you if your place is still bugged. But I beg you, Sue—beg you—to give me

one more chance, a last chance. You didn't mean what you said any more than I did. We love each other for keeps. It's as simple as that. Meet me at the Metropolitan Museum as soon as you can after you get this. Near the Vermeers. If necessary I'll wait until the place closes. Please, Sue. I'm not worth another chance, but be generous and give me one. I love you so much. Larry.

I don't believe I hesitated for a moment. This time I did not bother with any disguise. Instead I decided to rely on ingenuity. I put on my heavy winter coat with its fur lining and fur hood, checked to see that I had enough money, and let myself out of the house. When I passed Hart's door, I walked as softly as I could. For some reason I did not want to incur his disapproval for meeting Larry and, after giving me the letter, he would, of course, guess where I had gone. Like the children and the Pied Piper.

When I went down the stoop, I saw a couple of women, huddled in a doorway on the opposite side of the street, nudge each other and peer at me, but I went swiftly to the corner where I found a cab and drove to Macy's. Of all the places in New York Macy's was the one in which it should be easiest to lose myself, and I went up to the toy department. On the long escalator journey from floor to floor, looking down on the crowded aisles, I did not once turn back to see whether anyone was following me.

Once in the crowded toy department, I felt sure somehow that I was going to escape surveillance. This was one meeting with Larry that was not going to be monitored. Cautiously I edged my way toward the bank of elevators, waited until the door was about to close, and darted in, squeezing against an indignant woman who had several bulky packages in her arms. When we reached the main floor, I went out a side entrance and hailed another cab, giving the Metropolitan Museum as my destination.

It was a bright blue day and the stark branches in

Central Park were transformed by snow. Only on the ground did white city snow give way to filthy black city slush.

Hope was rising like an iridescent bubble by the time I reached the Met. For the first time the driver noticed me. "Hey, did anyone ever say you look like that model—you know the one?"

"I know the one." I gave him his fare and a tip and went running up the long flight of stairs to the entrance. It had been so long since I had visited the Met that I had to ask where the Vermeers were, and when I reached the right gallery, Larry was not there. I looked around uncertainly. A schoolteacher with a long file of children behind her was discussing Vermeer in a way guaranteed to make it impossible for any child ever again to look with pleasure at paintings. It was like the poor judgment that enthusiastically extols the virtues of spinach as opposed to lemon pie. A guard stood watching from the entrance to make sure that none of the children proved to be vandals.

The class moved on to another gallery to complete their educational inoculation against art, and the guard moved after them. It was then that Larry appeared, glanced warily around and came to take my hand. This time we could see each other clearly. I could see the difference that the months had made, see the new lines etched in his face, see how his faith in his world had been shaken as well as his faith in himself. This was a new Larry, wary and distrustful.

"I scrammed out of here when the kids came through because the guard was keeping an eye on everyone and I thought it would be as well not to be noticed in case any of the kids did any damage. The last thing I need now is to be called into court as a witness." His face lighted up. "Sue! I hoped you would come."

"You knew I would."

"Well—" His hand tightened. "Some things never change. Suppose we go wandering around this place like proper culture seekers. We've got to talk. There's so much to say."

"Did you know you were followed yesterday when you met me at the movie?"

I could see the shock in his face. "Good God! If I had known that I'd never have subjected you to such a thing. This is hell, Sue, absolute hell. We can't meet openly and yet we simply have to talk. And when we do, I make a fool of myself and say something so rotten I should have my tongue cut out and thrown to the cats."

"I said things too."

Larry cleared his throat and looked at me with the first uncertainty I'd ever seen in him. "Sue, how about this fellow Mullen? How does he stand with you?"

For reply I stripped off my gloves and showed him my ringless hand.

"Were you that sure, even after the way I acted?" He was shaken.

I nodded. After all, there wasn't much of anything that needed to be said. When Larry and I were together, it was like two halves being fitted together to make a complete person.

We strolled along galleries, paused to look at pictures. This time I felt sure there was no one following us. I explained how I had escaped by way of Macy's, in case it should be necessary to shake anyone off. I tried to make it sound funny, but Larry was not amused.

"As though we were criminals," he said angrily. "Sue, will you take me back? I can't do without you. I know that now. I haven't anything to offer you. The gallery isn't mine, you know. I have no job. Probably no university will take me. They don't need men on their faculty who have been involved in murder."

"We'll work it out somehow," I assured him. "But we'll have to wait until all this is cleared up so completely that no one can ever suspect either of us of being involved in Hope's death. We couldn't live with that."

"Sue, why did you write me that letter last spring?"

I told him why.

"Hope." There was an ugly tone in his voice.

"She really loved you, Larry. She may have lied about her heart condition as a—a kind of lever—but I think she was honest about loving you."

"I thought so too—in the beginning. But then—I must have been as conceited as they come. I assumed that a girl could go all out for me that way, giving me the gallery and all that."

"There was another girl who went all out," I reminded him, "though she didn't have anything to give." And, I told myself bitterly, Hope didn't give you the gallery.

"But that was different. That was you. You and me. The way it should be."

That afternoon we sauntered through the museum as though no one but ourselves was in that vast building. Now and then I was dimly aware of guards stationed at the entrance to the various galleries. Once, weary of walking, we sat down on a bench in a room devoted to impressionist paintings, the chief attraction being that the room was empty.

In a few minutes a heavy woman came in to settle herself in a businesslike way on the bench beside us and take out a sketchbook. The chief trouble about people like that is that they inevitably attract an audience. People hovered, looking from the original Matisse to the unconvincing sketch with the air of knowledgeable connoisseurs. A bald man with a trim Vandyke beard, puffy cheeks and pince-nez on a broad black ribbon—the first I had seen in years—stopped to examine her work with some contempt and then passed on.

Larry, watching the copyist critically, said, "She's wasting her time. She's no good and never will be. No eye at all."

"Just another artist *manqué* in the wrong vocation," I said idly.

"Or perhaps she has a different vocation."

"We're beginning to see bogeys everywhere," I told him.

173

After a time he checked his watch. "I suppose the police will be out looking for you if I keep you any longer. God knows when we'll have a chance to meet again. I hate this furtive business but, as long as they have any suspicions—"

"I know."

"The worst of it is that they aren't getting anywhere. They don't even seem to have a workable theory."

"Roger has a theory." I told him of Roger's belief that Phelps's death had been brought about by a sudden and violent shock, perhaps caused by a telephone call, and that somewhere there was a tape that recorded that conversation.

"But there's not a concrete fact in all that rigmarole," Larry said impatiently.

"Roger thinks Hope knew about the tape and took it. He thinks Winnie stole it from her as she tried to steal a gold compact. She was a lot like a magpie in some ways, you know."

"I know," Larry said grimly. "There was a real uproar one night when Phelps caught her prowling around the library. She said she was looking for something to read."

"Well, anyhow, Roger believes Winnie got the tape and hid it in her apartment, and her attacker failed to find it."

After a long and thoughtful pause Larry said, "It's a slim chance, of course, but anything is worth trying. Could you get into her apartment?"

"Oh, no, Larry! That would be too risky. About all either of us needs at this point is to be found trying to break into Winnie's apartment, the place where she was murdered. No, leave it to the police. They could do a much better job of searching than I possibly could."

"I won't buy that," Larry said.

"Why on earth not?"

"Because we don't know what may be on that tape. We aren't going to risk confiding in the police until we know where we are."

Chapter 15

Roger was not waiting for me when I got home. I had not expected him to be. He had known, the night before, that there was a barrier between us he could not tear down and I felt a pang of grief not only for him but for myself. I was going to miss him, miss his companionship, his lighthearted approach to life. He was always there when he was needed. Under his casual manner he was a rock to whom one could cling. And there had been moments—but I thrust those out of my mind. It was Larry whom I loved.

Thoughts of Larry brought me no comfort that night as I opened a can of soup and made a sandwich, too restless to settle down for a proper meal. It was because those meetings were stolen that they had felt so wrong, that I had reaped so little comfort from them. I recalled the happiness we had shared in the spring, but somehow I could not reconstruct it. Of course, with Hope's murder less than a week behind us, it was madness to think of trying to rebuild my former relationship with Larry. That belonged to the future. And at that moment I found it hard to believe in the remote future.

Meantime there was Larry's suggestion that I search Winnie's apartment. The idea was preposterous and potentially dangerous. Anyhow, even if I could get in, and there was no reason to think I could, the chances that I would find what her murderer had sought, what the police, trained in such operations, had sought and failed to find, was remote. I wished, not for the first time, that Larry had not balked at the idea of persuading the police to make another search of Winnie's apartment. There could not conceivably be anything on the tape—if it existed and if they found it—that could endanger Larry. Not possibly. But I wished, somehow, he had not been so emphatic about it.

In spite of revulsion and a sense of loyalty betrayed, I found myself thinking of the detective advising me to give Larry a wide berth. "People quite often come up with the right answer. It's not a difficult sum." I thought of Hart calling Larry a lady-killer. I remembered Roger calling him a heel.

All evening I vacillated. It wouldn't do any harm just to go up and try the door.—I was going to put the whole thing out of my mind.—If I could find the tape and help solve the mystery of the murders, Larry and I would be free of suspicion, free to marry.—If I were caught in Winnie's apartment, I'd be in worse trouble than I'd ever known in all my life.

It went on like that. I told myself firmly to forget it. I rinsed out some nylons and hung them over the shower rod, anything to occupy my hands if not my mind.

At no time did I consciously make a decision, but at eleven, without being aware of having made up my mind, I slipped off my shoes, unlocked my door as quietly as I could, and went swiftly up the stairs, wearing dark sweater and skirt. The hall was chilly as it had been since Higgins's departure, but there was not a sound in the building except for the television in Hart's apartment where someone was discussing new careers for men. Poor Hart having to start over again. It wasn't fair.

Outside Winnie's door I got my first feeling that this enterprise, after all, might be workable. There was no seal on the door, as I had half expected, and I knew that neither the bolt nor the chain could be in operation. Tentatively I tried my own key in the lock, but, of course, it didn't work. Then, armed with a credit card in its plastic cover, I used an idea I had seen in crime pictures. I slid the card into the crack in the door and pressed it slowly up and down. And then, considerably to my surprise, the lock moved and I was able to open the door.

My first thought was, "Why, it really works!" Then I closed the door and switched on the light in the living room.

No attempt had been made to restore order since the murder, the ransacking, and the police search. The place was an awful mess. Winnie had filled every available foot with chairs, tables, lamps. At best there had barely been space to move around in freely; one was always having to edge past a chair or table too big for the room. But now it looked as though a cyclone had struck it.

My first feeling was one of shame at intruding in this apartment which was not mine, where I had no right to be. My second feeling was an awareness that I was shaking—with cold, I thought, but it was fear. Only a few nights ago, someone had coaxed Winnie to open her door. Had she recognized her murderer? Had she known that she was to die as Hope had died?

I was thinking myself into a panic. *Cut it out,* I told myself. And get to work. Hurry.

I did not know where to start. I stood just inside the door, my eyes moving slowly around the room. Everything, absolutely everything, had been torn apart and searched. Nothing, so far as I could see, had been overlooked. Even the pictures hung askew as though someone had looked behind them. Chairs were tilted so someone could look underneath.

There were only a few books: the top best seller, because Winnie, having no taste of her own, liked to "keep up." There was a new sex novel that made me raise astonished eyebrows, and half a dozen of the more lurid paperbacks. On a magazine stand I found Winnie's real reading, the type of magazine devoted to libelous stories about celebrated people, the stuff that appeals to the peeping Tom and to the envious, who, since they cannot climb the ladder, try to saw through the rungs of those who can.

I went through Winnie's knitting bag, pricking my finger on one of the steel needles. In a gingerly way I thrust my arm up the chimney on the theory that if one flue held a cache the others might do so, but there was nothing, no loose bricks, nothing at all.

If anything was hidden in the apartment, it must be beyond my reach. There was no use in looking farther; I felt sure of that. I felt sure, too, that the sooner I got out, the better. But, as long as I had got this far, I went into the bedroom where I found the same disorder. Winnie's bed, like mine, like Hart's, had been torn apart, closets emptied, bureau drawers overturned. I climbed on a chair and felt along the top shelf of the closet, but there was nothing but some old hats and summer handbags Winnie had put away for the winter.

Her bedroom window, like mine, looked out on a court, a small, dark court with an ugly fire escape climbing up past the window. Beyond the brownstone was an office building with lights only on one floor where cleaning women were at work. I tried to unlock the window and discovered that it had not been fastened. Considering the multiple locks on the door, this was an incredible oversight. Unless this was how the murderer got in, perhaps attacking Winnie when she was half asleep and then letting himself out by the door. I pushed up the window and had a queer feeling that something moved, which was ridiculous. It was simply a shadow cast by my own body against the light.

My nerves were more on edge than I had realized. As I climbed out on the narrow landing, it seemed to me I felt a faint vibration as though someone were moving on the fire escape. I realized this was nothing but overstrained nerves; just the same, the impression remained, grew stronger, that I was not alone out there in the cold and dark.

This was the only chance I'd had to discover what— if anything—Winnie had concealed, the thing that had precipitated her murder.

I made myself grope over every inch of that landing, in case Winnie had put the tape out there for safekeeping. And my fingers touched something small and hard. Closed over it.

My heart was thumping like Poe's Telltale Heart while I crept back through the window and closed it. Eagerly I held my treasure under the light. My disappointment was so severe that I realized that, in spite of common sense, I had hoped to find something the police and a frantic murderer had missed. What I held in my hand was a lump of frozen mud, perhaps the size of an egg. Just mud! I dropped it in disgust.

Then I did a double-take. The weather had been severe, but it had not rained mud. Someone had been on that landing. Oh, of course, I realized belatedly, the police must have searched it as well as the apartment, and the frozen mud had dropped off the boots of one of them.

In Winnie's bathroom, too, it was obvious that nothing had been left for the inexpert hands of the amateur to find. I looked where others had looked, searched a dirty clothes hamper others had searched, searched the medicine cabinet, the toilet tank, and gave up.

I switched off the lights in the bedroom and bathroom and tackled the kitchen. That was my last chance. At least it was warmer than the bedroom, which had been cold even before I had opened the window. Here, too, the ransacking had been ruthless; certainly it had been needlessly destructive. After all, it was not necessary to break things, and yet quite a lot of things had been broken. It was as though the killer, thwarted in his search, had destroyed out of sheer vindictiveness.

I skirted the messy piles of sugar and flour and coffee on the floor and, after a despairing look around, climbed on the kitchen ladder and started at the top shelf of the cupboards, working my way down, feeling every inch of the shelves, looking in everything that had a cover, even prodding food packages that had been opened. I poked my fingers into stove burners and into the oven.

It was the hum of the refrigerator that made me turn to it as a last resort, after having gone through the unsavory business of prodding into a trash can and even the garbage pail, whose absence had led to Higgins's discovery of Winnie's murder.

There was little enough in the refrigerator. I'd noticed from the supply of canned goods that Winnie was no cook. I found milk and margarine but no butter or cream, because Winnie watched her calories. There was a congealed dish of spinach and a bowl of cold spaghetti, looking gluey, left over from some meal. She hadn't had much, I thought! Poor Winnie!

In the ice compartment there was nothing but the trays themselves. As a last gesture I pulled them out. One of them contained only ice cubes. The other held a dark purplish mess that puzzled me. Cautiously I tasted a tiny bit on the tip of a teaspoon. Frozen grape sherbet. But Winnie never ate desserts. Never.

For the first time since I had picked up that hunk of frozen mud on the landing I felt a rising excitement. I held the tray under hot water, watching while the thick, congealed mess slowly melted and dropped into the sink. There was a small metallic click. And there at last, closely wrapped in plastic to protect it, was the tape! At least, it must be the tape. Winnie would never have gone to such lengths to conceal what appeared to be merely a cigarette case. I was aware of cold air swirling around my ankles and turned hastily. Hart stood in the doorway, looking at me with incredulity and shock.

"You! Sue!" Anger throbbed in his voice. "Good God, woman, what's wrong with you? Prowling around this house where two women have been strangled, one of them right here in this apartment! What in hell are you doing? Can't the police make you understand that this isn't safe?"

"I know." I was too excited to mind his anger, which, after all, was only on my account. "I know, but I thought—that is, Larry thought—"

"Larry! Do you mean to tell me that bastard sent you up here alone tonight to search Winnie's apartment? If that doesn't give you a taste of his quality, I don't know what would."

"Wait, Hart, wait. It's all right, I tell you. It's all right."

"What is all right?" The anger faded as he looked at me more closely. "Sue, have you been drinking? Or—it isn't dope, is it?" And he looked as though I had turned into someone else.

"Oh, don't be absurd. I'm excited because I've found the tape."

"What tape?"

"The one Roger figured must be here. And Larry thought so too."

"What tape is that?" He came into the kitchen, walking carefully, as I had done, to avoid tramping in the mess of flour and sugar and coffee.

I showed it to him.

He looked at it, frowning, as I ripped off the plastic cover that had protected it from the grape sherbet. "It looks like a cigarette case. What makes you think it is so important?"

"Why else would Winnie have gone to the trouble of hiding it so carefully?"

"Where did you find it?"

"In one of the ice trays."

"But there was nothing—" He broke off.

My face was a dead giveaway, of course. For a long moment I stared at him and then I tried to edge unobtrusively toward the door, but Hart stood in the way, unmoving.

"I picked up a tape recorder today," he said. "Let's try this and find out what is really on it. It may be a mare's nest, you know, or it may have something you wouldn't want the police to hear."

That sounded enough like Larry to make me feel acutely uncomfortable. My hand closed more tightly over the tape. I continued to try to edge past Hart.

Then his hand shot out, seizing my wrist. "Sue! Wait a minute."

"Let me go, Hart."

"What's wrong?" he asked reproachfully. "What are you afraid of?" As I tried to free myself, his hand tightened. He was holding me against him now, twisted so that my back was to him, as it had been when the needle had gone into my arm.

"Hart!" It was hardly more than a whisper. "Hart! Please let me go. Please don't hurt me, Hart!"

"Quiet!" That was the whisper I had heard in my apartment.

They do these things better in the movies where the clear-headed, controlled heroine saves herself by brilliant acting or bluff, but I was too frightened to think. I was afraid to die, afraid of the pain, the choking. I had no pride at all.

"What are you going to do to me?" I was whimpering and past being ashamed.

"I didn't want to do anything to you, but you haven't left me much choice, have you? If you just hadn't snooped. You and Winnie."

"Winnie knew, didn't she? Or she guessed. I remember how she acted when I said she must have seen or heard something when Hope was killed. She must have heard your door close. And I can see now that she hesitated when I said it was the brooch Hope was coming to get. It was not only the brooch but the tape. Probably she took it for a pretty cigarette case and she couldn't resist it. And then she learned how important it was. But Hope—how could you kill Hope? You loved her."

"Yes, I loved her. I was old dog Tray. If she had only married me, everything would have been all right. Nothing would have gone wrong. God! I dream of her at night. Horrible dreams. She was so—so gentle and sweet in her ways, until she asked me to be Larry's best man. She liked that touch. She kept me at the apartment where I had to watch her glowing at Larry. From the time she married him, my position was insecure. If she had been my wife, Phelps would have stuck to me through thick and thin. You never really knew Phelps, did you? No one did except for Hope and me. He was a calculating bastard. He always made sure of people, one way and another. With me it was my marriage to Hope that would keep me loyal."

"So you knew about him all along."

"I knew all along," Hart admitted. "I helped him build the pyramid block by block. But after Hope's marriage, he tried, like a fool, to short-change me. And, what with one thing and another, that was too much. I said if I didn't get my cut, I'd expose him. I had enough on him to send him to the pen for life and he knew it. The Gray Eminence would be shown up as just a common criminal. He told me I couldn't expose him without incriminating myself. He pointed out that I'd already had a nice fat sum out of him and he told me in what banks I had safety deposit boxes and under what names I had rented them. If I opened my mouth, he'd take me down with him, for income tax evasion if on no other charge."

A vein in Hart's temple was swollen and throbbed with anger. "We'd never before exchanged so much as an angry word and this was a real battle. I told him that when people knew the part he had played in Graham Woods's suicide, he would be pilloried, that Woods had been the kind of guy he had always wanted people to think he was. He didn't like that but he smiled at me—you know that way he had of smiling that made you feel like two cents—"

"I never saw him like that." The words didn't mean anything, just postponing the moment when, his fury exhausted, he would dispose of me. Even one more minute was worth hoping for.

"Well, I sort of lunged at him. I swear I didn't mean to touch him. I fact, I didn't touch him. He said, in that slow way of his, as though nothing ever hurried or flurried him, 'You fool, do you think I haven't had your number all the time? Every word of this conversation is being recorded where you'll never find it, so I'd advise you against attempting any violence." And he sat looking at me and smiling and then he grabbed his chest and toppled over.

183

"I called Hope and we went through that library as fast as we could, getting rid of any evidence we knew of. It was Hope who thought of unlocking the library door in case any question about missing files came up. That's when she told me about the tapes that had recorded every business talk Phelps had had in the place. And then she reached in his jacket pocket and pulled out that cigarette case which he always carried. She said it was especially made and that it might well have recorded his last words and she wanted it as a memento."

"So Phelps didn't ever trust you. He never told you about the tapes; he never told you about the cache of money in the chimney." I added, "He really did have your number."

Hart didn't like that.

"But who knocked you out?"

"Oh, I did that myself, after I'd taken care of Winnie and set the stage in my apartment." He looked at the tape I still clung to, his face darkening. "Hidden in an ice tray! What a lousy female trick."

"How did you?" I persisted.

"How did I what? Oh, knock myself out? I hit my head as hard as I could with that heavy granite paperweight. You'd be surprised to know how difficult it is to knock yourself out deliberately. Part of you simply refuses to obey orders. Like making yourself put a finger down on a hot stove. It won't go."

"But it didn't refuse to let you kill Hope, did it? Was it fun, Hart, waiting for her with a noose in your hand, a noose to go around that soft little throat?"

"Stop that! God, do you think I liked it? But she called me. She said she was coming here to retrieve the tape. She said she'd already listened to it. She said anyone hearing it would believe by the abrupt way it ended that I had been responsible for Phelps's heart attack. She believed that herself."

"But her father had been dead for weeks!"

"She hadn't listened to the tape before. She had suspected for a while that Larry had caused that attack." Hart laughed shortly.

"Well, I had encountered Hope's ruthlessness before. I knew she meant what she said. She meant me to suffer for her father's death. I doubt if the police could have held me for murder but on income tax evasion— that meant prison. God, I have claustrophobia, Sue! I'd go mad if I went to prison. So I made the noose and waited in that dark corner of the hall until she came. And—afterwards, I carried her up to that spot where there's a hole in the carpet and dropped her there so people would assume she had been going upstairs."

Somewhere something moved and I stood, tense, trying to figure out where it was, what it was.

Hart's hands were sliding around my throat. "Hart!" That scream tore out of my throat like a policeman's whistle. Or was there a policeman's whistle?

"Okay, Adams," a deep voice said, and then the room was filled with men. "Hands on top of your head. That's right. Now turn around nice and easy. All right. Handcuffs there. Miss," he turned to where I had sagged against the kitchen sink, "are you all right?"

"I guess so."

"Better turn over that little gadget to me, hadn't you?" The policeman took the tape from my unresisting hand. "Such a small thing to cause the death of two women and darned near a third one. Hey, boys, take him away and book him for Murder One. And don't neglect the usual warning. We don't want any bellyaching about his rights."

As the little procession moved out of the kitchen with Hart stumbling between two uniformed men, Roger came to take me in his arms.

"All right, Sue," he said. "All right."

"How did you get here?"

"I got to thinking about my fat-headed darling and what she was likely to do, though it seemed unlikely that you'd try to do it alone."

"Well, Larry thought—" I began.

185

"It was his idea?" Roger shook his head. "You are what in the theater is called a slow study. Come on, darling. There will be plenty of time for post-mortems tomorrow."

Epilogue

Roger was wrong about that. There was time for nothing in the days that followed but interminable interviews with the police, the FBI, the district attorney's office. There was no more mystery, unless a man's capacity for violence in order to achieve his goal is a mystery.

It was something of an anticlimax to know that, aside from the night when Hart had doped me, I had been in no danger at all. There had been five interested witnesses to Hart's talk with me in Winnie's kitchen. In fact, I had been chaperoned all along without being aware of it, not entirely on my account but because the police were still suspicious of some complicity between Larry and me. Larry had been followed to the theater where he met me and also to the Metropolitan Museum by the incompetent woman copyist who was a competent policewoman.

And there had been police in the building the night Hart tried to strangle me. Men across the street, in the court, in the lower hall, and on the fire escape. Roger had sold them his idea of the tape still existing somewhere in Winnie's apartment and they had arrived to make another search when they saw the lights go on in her living room as I went in. The man on the fire escape had cursed me roundly as he tried to climb out of sight without making any noise. No wonder I had felt so strongly that I was not alone!

It was only after considerable persuasion that they had agreed to let Roger go along, and then only on the understanding that he would not interfere. But when Hart had threatened me, they had to restrain him by force.

After the noise and confusion as the building down the block was being demolished, it was almost a relief to testify in quieter surroundings. When that building was gone, the next would go and the next until only the brownstone remained, stripped now of its secrets. The small fortune found in the chimney was negligible as American incomes go. It was small in comparison with the amounts acquired by minor politicians in lining their pockets at the public expense. Marshall Phelps had wielded immense power and acquired great prestige and yet he had little to show for so much chicanery and bribery and blackmail. The curious part was that with his personality, his ability, his capacity for almost mesmerizing people into believing in him, Marshall Phelps might have made millions by honest means. I suppose the idea never occurred to him.

The tape, of course, was completely damning when it was used against Hart not only in the Grand Jury hearings but in his trial. The discovery that Phelps and his faithful henchman had driven Graham Woods to suicide for the sum of $250,000 came as a tremendous shock to the public.

Hart, I believe, had begun to see himself as a kind of heir to the throne, an ambition that came to an abrupt end when Hope fell in love with Larry and married him. After that the partnership began to fray badly. The two men had lost their chief hold on each other and they had nothing left but a kind of mutual distrust.

I had one talk with Higgins, an unexpectedly formal and alert young FBI agent, when he came to apologize for having suspected me for a time of being the prowler on the fourth floor. "But you did look so guilty when I found you there." He added with a rather mischievous grin, "But I felt I owed you something, so I erased one of those tapes."

I could feel the color burning in my cheeks, but I said only "Thank you," and let it go.

Against his lawyer's advice Hart took the stand, though hardly in his own defense. At that point he had nothing to lose. His dream of a dazzling career in the Phelps manner had ended. The money in his safety deposit boxes—and incidentally he had more than Phelps—was retrieved as well as some correspondence which was not made public but which kept the police busy for a long time. He had killed Hope for his own safety and discovered that his life had no value without her.

About Winnie's murder he seemed to feel only indifference and a kind of resentment that she had outwitted him by concealing the tape.

I had been his last chance at finding it and he had decided, by then, to provide another suspect for the police. Any possibility of suspicion falling on Larry had ended when he learned that Larry had been in jail at the time of Winnie's murder. I had been Winnie's friend and Hope's and I had been in love with Hope's husband. I lived in the house where the crimes had been committed. I was the perfect patsy. With the only smile anyone observed on his face during the course of the trial Hart declared that the task of undressing me had been the high point of the whole affair. Roger, sitting beside me in the courtroom, had to be restrained by the firm hand of a policeman, seated beside him for just such a contingency.

In all this time I saw Larry only once, entering the district attorney's office when I was leaving it. We had no opportunity at all to talk and he did not call me, though I got one note saying he was keeping away until the mess had cleared up. For both our sakes. It was not until Hart was formally charged with murder that Larry arrived at my apartment.

Fear, now pointless, still left a kind of memory and I hesitated before I opened the door.

"Sue? It's Larry."

I let him in and he came to take me in his arms, crushing me against him. For a moment I stood still, without moving, and then, gently, I released myself.

"It began to seem like forever," he said. "Oh, Sue, thank God it's over and we can be together at last. I need you. I need you so awfully."

And nothing happened at all. I just didn't care any more. I saw his old smile, heard the fervor in his voice, and it didn't matter. I didn't dislike him. I could never do that. But the magic was gone. I had wanted support—how I had wanted it! But that was what Larry had wanted, too. He needed me. He had let me run into danger while he had waited in the wings for me to provide the action. He still had glamour, whatever that is, more than any man I had ever known, but the bond between us had been severed without my feeling a pang.

I saw the doubt growing in his face, doubt and a kind of shock. "Sue?"

Before I could speak, someone else knocked and I admitted Roger. The two men nodded to each other politely enough, but each with the undeniable air of saying, "Get out of here. We can get along without you."

And then Roger touched me lightly on the shoulder. "Okay?"

"Fine."

"You need someone to look after you. Is that what this guy has been telling you?"

"No," I said slowly, "he's been telling me that he needs someone to look after him."

Larry looked from one to the other. He was very white. Then he said in a colorless voice, "I seem to have made a mistake. All the best, Sue. Take care of her, Mullen."

When he had gone, I said, "It was cruel but I had to do it."

"Of course you had to."

"What will become of him, Roger?"

"There will always be some woman to pick up the pieces for Lawrence Garland. And you'll always be a little bit in love with him. Damn his soul!" And we said nothing more about Larry.

Hope's estate was soon cleared up. She had left everything to her "beloved husband." The money in the chimney, of course, was part of the tangled effects of Marshall Phelps, but when the brownstone house had been sold for an extortionate price as well as the Fifth Avenue duplex, there was enough money for Larry to continue running the art gallery, which he now owned.

"But he won't want to," I exclaimed in distress to Roger. "He doesn't like money. He doesn't want to collect moss."

"But that," Roger pointed out, "was before he knew the comfort and the advantage of having an ample supply of money. Believe me, he is going to enjoy it to the full."

Roger was right, of course. In his lighthearted way he is usually right. Just a month ago I received a card of invitation to a preview of a collection of post-impressionist paintings Larry was holding. A very plush affair with champagne for the invited guests—and potential buyers. He had acquired paintings on a trip, which had combined a honeymoon with a buying expedition. His wife is somewhat older than he, but she has an impressive amount of money and she is backing the gallery.

I wasn't able to attend the preview because Roger and I were at last making a tour of the Scandinavian countries. Working together was proving to be even more satisfying and rewarding than we had anticipated. And love-making was all that Roger had assured me it would be. We have proved that marriage can be a real partnership.

Yesterday Roger showed me a story in the Sunday paper, a rehash of the old nonsense about the "aura" of the brownstone house which had incited to violence. Now the house was being torn down. In a few weeks there would be no trace of it. In a few years, with a thirty-story high-rise apartment building in its place, few people would remember that it had ever been there.

But the shot that had destroyed Graham Woods no

longer echoed. If he failed to achieve his ambition of becoming President of the United States and a great public servant, his death accomplished almost as much. An ugly conspiracy to control public moneys through corrupt public officials had been brought to an end and the public had learned to know where the fatal weaknesses lay in the structure of government and how to prevent the depredations of future vultures. As a good citizen, perhaps Graham Woods would have voted it well worth while.